HIDDEN MAGIC

DRAGON'S GIFT SERIES STARTER

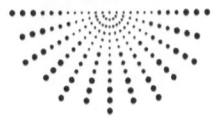

LINSEY HALL

For my readers. Thank you for everything!

CHAPTER ONE

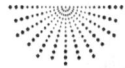

Jungle, Southeast Asia
Five years before the events in Ancient Magic

"How much are we being paid for this job again?" I glanced at the dudes filling the bar. It was a motley crowd of supernaturals, many of whom looked shifty as hell.

"Not nearly enough for one as dangerous as this." Del frowned at the man across the bar, who was giving her his best sexy face. There was a lot of eyebrow movement happening. "Is he having a seizure?"

"Looks like it." Nix grinned. "Though I gotta say, I wasn't expecting this. We're basically in a tree, for magic's sake. In the middle of the jungle! Where are all these dudes coming from?"

"According to my info, there's a mining operation near here. Though I'd say we're more *under* a tree than *in* a tree."

"I'm with Cass," Del said. "Under, not in."

"Fair enough," Nix said.

We were deep in Southeast Asia, in a bar that had long ago been reclaimed by the jungle. A massive fig tree had grown over and around the ancient building, its huge roots strangling the stone walls. It was straight out of a fairy tale.

Monks had once lived here, but a few supernaturals of indeterminate species had gotten ahold of it and turned it into a watering hole for the local supernaturals. We were meeting our contact here, but he was late.

"Hey, pretty lady." A smarmy voice sounded from my left. "What are you?"

I turned to face the guy who was giving me the up and down, his gaze roving from my tank top to my shorts. He wasn't Clarence, our local contact. And if he meant "what kind of supernatural are you?" I sure as hell wouldn't be answering. That could get me killed.

"Not interested is what I am," I said.

"Aww, that's no way to treat a guy." He grabbed my hip, rubbed his thumb up and down.

I smacked his hand away, tempted to throat-punch him. It was my favorite move, but I didn't want to start a fight before Clarence got here. Didn't want to piss off our boss.

The man raised his hands. "Hey, hey. No need to get feisty. You three sisters?"

I glanced at Nix and Del, at their dark hair that was so different from my red. We were all about twenty, but we looked nothing alike. And while we might call ourselves sisters—*deirfiúr* in our native Irish—this idiot didn't know that.

"Go away." I had no patience for dirt bags who touched me without asking. "Run along and flirt with your hand, because that's all the action you'll be getting tonight."

His face turned a mottled red, and he raised a fist. His magic welled, the scent of rotten fruit overwhelming.

He thought he was going to smack me? Or use his magic against me?

Ha.

I lashed out, punching him in the throat. His eyes bulged and he gagged. I kneed him in the crotch, grinning when he keeled over.

"Hey!" A burly man with a beard lunged for us, his buddy beside him following. "That's no way—"

"To treat a guy?" I finished for him as I kicked out at him. My tall, heavy boots collided with his chest, sending him flying backward. I never used my magic—didn't want to go to jail and didn't want to blow things up—but I sure as hell could fight.

His friend raised his hand and sent a blast of wind at us. It threw me backward, sending me skidding across the floor.

By the time I'd scrambled to my feet, a brawl had broken out in the bar. Fists flew left and right, with a bit of magic thrown in. Nothing bad enough to ruin the bar, like jets of flame, because no one wanted to destroy the only watering hole for a hundred miles, but enough that it lit up the air with varying magical signatures.

Nix conjured a baseball bat and swung it at a burly guy who charged her, while Del teleported behind a horned demon and smashed a chair over his head. I'd always been jealous of Del's ability to sneak up on people like that.

All in all, it was turning into a good evening. A fight between supernaturals was fun.

"Enough!" the bartender bellowed. "Or no more beer!"

The patrons quieted immediately. Fights might be fun, but they weren't worth losing beer over.

I glared at the jerk who'd started it. There was no way I'd take the blame, even though I'd thrown the first punch. He should have known better.

The bartender gave me a look and I shrugged, hiking a thumb at the jerk who'd touched me. "He shoulda kept his hands to himself."

"Fair enough," the bartender said.

I nodded and turned to find Nix and Del. They'd grabbed our

beers and were putting them on a table in the corner. I went to join them.

We were a team. Sisters by choice, ever since we'd woken in a field at fifteen with no memories other than those that said we were FireSouls on the run from someone who had hurt us. Who was hunting us.

Our biggest goal, even bigger than getting out from under our current boss's thumb, was to save enough money to buy conceal-ment charms that would hide us from the monster who hunted us. He was just a shadowy memory, but it was enough to keep us running.

"Where is Clarence, anyway?" I pulled my damp tank top away from my sweaty skin. The jungle was damned hot. We couldn't break into the temple until Clarence gave us the infor-mation we needed to get past the guard at the front. And we didn't need to spend too much longer in this bar.

Del glanced at her watch, her blue eyes flashing with annoy-ance. "He's twenty minutes late. Old Man Bastard said he should be here at eight."

Old Man Bastard—OMB for short—was our boss. His name said it all. Del, Nix, and I were FireSouls, the most despised species of supernatural because we could steal other magical being's powers if we killed them. We'd never done that, of course, but OMB didn't care. He'd figured out our secret when we were too young to hide it effectively and had been blackmailing us to work for him ever since.

It'd been four years of finding and stealing treasure on his behalf. Treasure hunting was our other talent, a gift from the dragon with whom legend said we shared a soul. No one had seen a dragon in centuries, so I wasn't sure if the legend was even true, but dragons were covetous, so it made sense they had a knack for finding treasure.

"What are we after again?" Nix asked.

"A pair of obsidian daggers," Del said. "Nice ones."

"And how much is this job worth?" Nix repeated my earlier question. Money was always on our minds. It was our only chance at buying our freedom, but OMB didn't pay us enough for it to be feasible anytime soon. We kept meticulous track of our earnings and saved like misers anyway.

"A thousand each."

"Damn, that's pathetic." I slouched back in my chair and stared up at the ceiling, too bummed about our crappy pay to even be impressed by the stonework and vines above my head.

"Hey, pretty ladies." The oily voice made my skin crawl. We just couldn't get a break in here. I looked up to see Clarence, our contact.

Clarence was a tall man, slender as a vine, and had the slicked back hair and pencil-thin mustache of a 1940s movie star. Unfortunately, it didn't work on him. Probably because his stare was like a lizard's. He was more Gomez Addams than Clark Gable. I'd bet anything that he liked working for OMB.

"Hey, Clarence," I said. "Pull up a seat and tell us how to get into the temple."

Clarence slid into a chair, his movement eerily snakelike. I shivered and scooted my chair away, bumping into Del. The scent of her magic flared, a clean hit of fresh laundry, as she no doubt suppressed her instinct to transport away from Clarence. If I had her gift of teleportation, I'd have to repress it as well.

"How about a drink first?" Clarence said.

Del growled, but Nix interjected, her voice almost nice. She had the most self control out of the three of us. "No can do, Clarence. You know... Mr. Oribis"—her voice tripped on the name, probably because she wanted to call him OMB—"wants the daggers soon. Maybe next time, though."

"Next time." Clarence shook his head like he didn't believe her. He might be a snake, but he was a clever one. His chest puffed up a bit. "You know I'm the only one who knows how to get into the temple. How to get into any of the places in this jungle."

"And we're so grateful you're meeting with us. Mr. Oribis is so grateful." Nix dug into her pocket and pulled out the crumpled envelope that contained Clarence's pay. We'd counted it and found—unsurprisingly—that it was more than ours combined, even though all he had to do was chat with us for two minutes. I'd wanted to scream when I'd seen it.

Clarence's gaze snapped to the money. "All right, all right."

Apparently his need to be flattered went out the window when cash was in front of his face. Couldn't blame him, though. I was the same way.

"So, what are we up against?" I asked.

The temple containing the daggers had been built by supernaturals over a thousand years ago. Like other temples of its kind, it was magically protected. Clarence's intel would save us a ton of time and damage to the temple if we could get around the enchantments rather than breaking through them.

"Dvarapala. A big one."

"A gatekeeper?" I'd seen one of the giant, stone monster statues at another temple before.

"Yep." He nodded slowly. "Impossible to get through. The temple's as big as the Titanic—hidden from humans, of course—but no one's been inside in centuries, they say."

Hidden from humans was a given. They had no idea supernaturals existed, and we wanted to keep it that way.

"So how'd you figure out the way in?" Del asked. "And why *haven't* you gone in? Bet there's lots of stuff you could fence in there. Temples are usually full of treasure."

"A bit of pertinent research told me how to get in. And I'd rather sell the entrance information and save my hide. It won't be easy to get past the booby traps in there."

Hide? Snakeskin, more like. Though he had a point. I didn't think he'd last long trying to get through a temple on his own.

"So? Spill it," I said, anxious to get going.

He leaned in, and the overpowering scent of cologne and sweat hit me. I grimaced, held my breath, then leaned forward to hear his whispers.

As soon as Clarence walked away, the communications charms around my neck vibrated. I jumped, then groaned. Only one person had access to this charm.

I shoved the small package Clarence had given me into my short's pocket and pressed my fingertips to the comms charm, igniting its magic.

"Hello, Mr. Oribis." I swallowed my bile at having to be polite.

"Girls," he grumbled.

Nix made a gagging face. We hated when he called us girls.

"Change of plans. You need to go to the temple tonight."

"What? But it's dark. We're going tomorrow." He never changed the plans on us. This was weird.

"I need the daggers sooner. Go tonight."

My mind raced. "The jungle is more dangerous in the dark. We'll do it if you pay us more."

"Twice the usual," Del said.

A tinny laugh echoed from the charm. "Pay *you* more? You're lucky I pay you at all."

I gritted my teeth and said, "But we've been working for you for four years without a raise."

"And you'll be working for me for four more years. And four after that. And four after that." Annoyance lurked in his tone. So did his low opinion of us.

Del's and Nix's brows crinkled in distress. We'd always suspected that OMB wasn't planning to let us buy our freedom, but he'd dangled that carrot in front of us. What he'd just said made that seem like a big fat lie, though. One we could add to the many others he'd told us.

An urge to rebel, to stand up to the bully who controlled our lives, seethed in my chest.

"No," I said. "You treat us like crap, and I'm sick of it. Pay us fairly."

"I treat you like *crap,* as you so eloquently put it, because that is exactly what you are. *FireSouls.*" He spit the last word, imbuing it with so much venom I thought it might poison me.

I flinched, frantically glancing around to see if anyone in the bar had heard what he'd called us. Fortunately, they were all distracted. That didn't stop my heart from thundering in my ears as rage replaced the fear. I opened my mouth to shout at him, but snapped it shut. I was too afraid of pissing him off.

"Get it by dawn," he barked. "Or I'm turning one of you in to the Order of the Magica. Prison will be the least of your worries. They might just execute you."

I gasped. "You wouldn't." Our government hunted and imprisoned—or destroyed—FireSouls.

"Oh, I would. And I'd enjoy it. The three of you have been more trouble than you're worth. You're getting cocky, thinking you have a say in things like this. Get the daggers by dawn, or one of you ends up in the hands of the Order."

My skin chilled, and the floor felt like it had dropped out from under me. He was serious.

"Fine." I bit off the end of the word, barely keeping my voice from shaking. "We'll do it tonight. Del will transport them to you as soon as we have them."

"Excellent." Satisfaction rang in his tone, and my skin crawled. "Don't disappoint me, or you know what will happen."

The magic in the charm died. He'd broken the connection.

I collapsed back against the chair. In times like these, I wished I had it in me to kill. Sure, I offed demons when they came at me on our jobs, but that was easy because they didn't actually die. Killing their earthly bodies just sent them back to their hell.

But I couldn't kill another supernatural. Not even OMB. It might get us out of this lifetime of servitude, but I didn't have it in me. And what if I failed? I was too afraid of his rage—and the consequences—if I didn't succeed.

"Shit, shit, shit." Nix's green eyes were stark in her pale face. "He means it."

"Yeah." Del's voice shook. "We need to get those daggers."

"Now," I said.

"I wish I could just conjure a forgery," Nix said. "I really don't want to go out into the jungle tonight. Getting past the Dvarapala in the dark will suck."

Nix was a conjurer, able to create almost anything using just her magic. Massive or complex things, like airplanes or guns, were outside of her ability, but a couple of daggers wouldn't be hard.

Trouble was, they were a magical artifact, enchanted with the ability to return to whoever had thrown them. Like boomerangs. Though Nix could conjure the daggers, we couldn't enchant them.

"We need to go. We only have six hours until dawn." I grabbed my short swords from the table and stood, shoving them into the holsters strapped to my back.

A hush descended over the crowded bar.

I stiffened, but the sound of the staticky TV in the corner made me relax. They weren't interested in me. Just the news, which was probably being routed through a dozen techno-witches to get this far into the jungle.

The grave voice of the female reporter echoed through the quiet bar. "The FireSoul was apprehended outside of his apartment in Magic's Bend, Oregon. He is currently in the custody of the Order of the Magica, and his trial is scheduled for tomorrow morning. My sources report that execution is possible."

I stifled a crazed laugh. Perfect timing. Just what we needed to hear after OMB's threat. A reminder of what would happen if he turned us into the Order of the Magica. The hush that had descended over the previously rowdy crowd—the kind of hush you get at the scene of a big accident—indicated what an interesting freaking topic this was. FireSouls were the bogeymen. *I* was the bogeyman, even though I didn't use my powers. But as long as no one found out, we were safe.

My gaze darted to Del and Nix. They nodded toward the door. It was definitely time to go.

As the newscaster turned her report toward something more boring and the crowd got rowdy again, we threaded our way between the tiny tables and chairs.

I shoved the heavy wooden door open and sucked in a breath of sticky jungle air, relieved to be out of the bar. Night creatures screeched, and moonlight filtered through the trees above. The jungle would be a nice place if it weren't full of things that wanted to kill us.

"We're never escaping him, are we?" Nix said softly.

"We will." Somehow. Someday. "Let's just deal with this for now."

We found our motorcycles, which were parked in the lot with a dozen other identical ones. They were hulking beasts with massive, all-terrain tires meant for the jungle floor. We'd done a lot of work in Southeast Asia this year, and these were our favored forms of transportation in this part of the world.

Del could transport us, but it was better if she saved her power. It wasn't infinite, though it did regenerate. But we'd learned a long time ago to save Del's power for our escape. Nothing worse than being trapped in a temple with pissed off guardians and a few tripped booby traps.

We'd scouted out the location of the temple earlier that day, so we knew where to go.

I swung my leg over Secretariat—I liked to name my vehicles

—and kicked the clutch. The engine roared to life. Nix and Del followed, and we peeled out of the lot, leaving the dingy yellow light of the bar behind.

Our headlights illuminated the dirt road as we sped through the night. Huge fig trees dotted the path on either side, their twisted trunks and roots forming an eerie corridor. Elephant-ear sized leaves swayed in the wind, a dark emerald that gleamed in the light.

Jungle animals howled, and enormous lightning bugs flitted along the path. They were too big to be regular bugs, so they were most likely some kind of fairy, but I wasn't going to stop to investigate. There were dangerous creatures in the jungle at night —one of the reasons we hadn't wanted to go now—and in our world, fairies could be considered dangerous.

Especially if you called them lightning bugs.

A roar sounded in the distance, echoing through the jungle and making the leaves rustle on either side as small animals scurried for safety.

The roar came again, only closer.

Then another, and another.

"Oh shit," I muttered. This was bad.

CHAPTER TWO

"Big cats coming!" Del called.

The roars sounded closer. I gave the bike some gas and crouched low over the handlebars. The engine rumbled, and the bike surged forward.

I didn't want to get caught by the Big Mousers, as the locals jokingly called the enormous cats that stalked the jungle. They were twice as big as a normal jaguar and as fast as my bike. Though they weren't demon felines, they were magical. Bigger, faster, and stronger than your average panther or jaguar. I'd never seen them outside of this jungle.

Thundering paws thudded over the sound of my bike's engine. I turned to look. Four massive black cats chased us, their golden eyes glowing with magic. Their fur was sleek and black, and long, white fangs peaked out of mouths that looked to be grinning.

Magical animals knew not to appear to humans—it was an instinct honed over thousands of generations. Just like supernaturals knew to stay under the radar of humans, so did the smarter supernatural animal species. That was why they were still alive instead of extinct, unlike unicorns. Those horned idiots had been pretty, but dumb. They'd revealed themselves to humans, then boom! Extinct.

But when a magical animal got an opportunity to hunt a supernatural, they took it. We were fair game. And for the most part, we wouldn't kill them out of principle alone. I certainly wouldn't. Which was why it was such a pain to run into them.

"Nix!" I shouted as I turned back to the road just in time to dodge a fallen tree limb.

"On it!" Her magic swelled in the air, the scent of flowers competing with the humid jungle smell.

When I glanced back around, I saw her conjure an enormous steak and toss it over her shoulder. One of the cats veered off, snagging it out of the air.

I winced as its jaws clamped down, then turned back to the road. If I crashed, my bike would trip up Del's and Nix's, then we'd be kitty chow.

Nix's magic swelled in the air three more times. Each time I glanced back to see a cat veer off with a steak clamped between its jaws.

But the final cat—the biggest—just swallowed it whole and kept running, paws pounding the ground and eyes intent on us. He just looked like he wanted to chase.

Perfect.

"I can conjure a whole dead cow, but it'll use up a lot of my power!" Nix shouted.

That wouldn't be good, not when we would need it for the temple.

"We're almost there!" I shouted.

Magic vibrated in the air. The big cat's footsteps slowed. I turned back. He roared, his fangs like daggers.

We'd crossed over the threshold of the temple's land. He didn't like the magic, thank fates, so he wouldn't come any farther. And in fairness, he had just had dinner. At this point, he was just being greedy by wanting to chew on my head.

A moment later, the huge gate appeared. Massive walls extended on either side, stretching deep into the jungle. We pulled our bikes to a stop in front of the expansive stone stairs that led up to the gate.

It was one of the biggest buildings I'd ever seen, so large that we were probably just looking at the exterior guard walls. The temple would be in the huge courtyard behind the walls. I'd seen other temples with that layout, all of which had been smaller than this place.

Moonlight illuminated the structure. Intricately carved, dome-shaped towers reached for the sky, their elegant forms extending above the treetops. We were in Southeast Asia, so some of the artistic and construction influences had been Buddhist and Hindu, but the supernaturals themselves hadn't necessarily practiced those religions. Which was good, because I didn't like to mess with human holy places. And this place was far from human. Magic radiated from the temple, a prickling sensation that filled the air and made the hair on my arms stand up.

We climbed off our bikes and turned them off.

"There's a force field over the wall," Del said. "See the light?"

I squinted, finally able to make out the vague glow that hovered over the walls like a dome.

"Protects the inner courtyard, I bet," I said.

"Along with that guy." Nix pointed at the sweeping staircase leading up to the sculpture of a giant wielding a club.

The Dvarapala.

We wouldn't be going over the walls because of the magic, so we'd have to go through him.

The statue was beautiful, in a terrifying way, with an intricately carved crown propped on his head. He guarded the only entrance to the massive temple, his huge stone form blocking the way. We could have tried blasting through him with magic, but it would have taken more power than we had. And I hated to hurt ancient sites like these. It just seemed wrong to destroy something that had been here a thousand years before I was even born.

I tugged the package Clarence had given me out of my pocket and unfolded the paper. A crumpled blossom lay inside, its scent strong and sweet.

"I'll wake him up if you want to do the honors," Del said.

I nodded. According to Clarence, one was supposed to wake the Dvarapala and convince him of your worthiness to enter. We definitely weren't worthy, so the next best thing was to drug him with the Oridian Orchid. Theoretically, for the period of time that the Dvarapala was awake, he was in human form. He would be susceptible to the flower's poison and fall right asleep.

Only problem was that he was fifteen feet tall and probably weighed two thousand pounds.

"I'll help you," Nix said.

"Cool." I carefully tucked the orchid into the pocket of my shorts, then set off for the stairs, Nix and Del at my side.

We climbed the stairs, taking them two at a time, until we reached the landing. Vines climbed up the walls, and intricate carvings of people and animals peeked through. They probably told some kind of story, but I had no idea what kind.

The Dvarapala loomed overhead, his impassive stone gaze glued to the jungle behind us. In the distance, one of the Big Mousers roared, sending a shiver across my spine.

"This place feels weird," I said, reaching over my shoulder to grasp my sword handle. I didn't draw it, just held it for comfort. Like a teddy bear. A very sharp teddy bear.

"Creepy, is what it feels like," Del said, then set off to look for the switch to awaken the Dvarapala.

I studied the covered landing that we stood upon, trying to figure out the best way to sneak up on a giant and shove something into his mouth.

My job definitely deserved hazard pay.

"Can you conjure a rope attached to the ceiling?" I asked Nix.

The ceiling had to be at least thirty feet high, supported by huge pillars decorated with carvings of dancing women. Tall enough for our plan. There were no wooden beams or anything, but there were massive carvings leering down at us.

She glanced up, then pointed to an elephant head that protruded from the ceiling. "Sure. I can put it around that elephant trunk."

"Found it!" Del gestured to us from where she stood near the giant's left leg. Her head only reached his thigh.

Nix and I joined her.

She pointed at the outline of a handprint carved into the giant's thigh. "That's it, I think."

"Yep," I said.

"Let me conjure the rope first." Nix held out her hand, her expression intense. Her magic swelled in the air, wrapping around me. The delicate scent of flowers filled my nose and I felt water lapping at my skin. Everyone's signature was different, and I liked to think that good people had nice signatures, though I didn't know if it was true.

Unlike Del and Nix, I didn't use my magic. I was a Mirror Mage, able to mimic any nearby supernatural's magic, but I had a bad habit of blowing stuff up when I tried. From the size of my explosions, I was probably a pretty strong Mirror Mage. Other supernaturals were always interested in strong magic, and it was really suspicious that I hadn't gotten a handle on mine. I was twenty, for magic's sake, with all the control of a two-year-old storm witch. Since I didn't want to blow things up or alert people to my weirdness—and perhaps set them on the path to discovering I was a FireSoul—there was no magic for me.

Nix's hand began to glow. A rope appeared, coiled at her feet. She tied a loop around the end, then threw it so it caught on the elephant's tusk above. Nix handed the dangling end to me.

I grabbed it. "Thanks."

"Ready?" Del asked.

"Almost." I draped the rope over my shoulder, then turned and climbed up the wall to the right of the stone giant, using the vines as a handhold. I did my best to stay off the carvings. They looked sturdy, but even stone could break.

Nix ducked behind the other side of the giant. "You know, seeing you up there, this suddenly doesn't seem like the brightest plan."

"Our plans are always bright," I said.

"Yeah, not exactly," Del said.

"But they're almost always successful," Nix said.

"Here's to another one." I was a few feet higher than the giant's head, so I stopped climbing and braced myself, then pulled the rope until it was taut. I dug the flower out of my pocket and carefully gripped it in my palm.

Actually, in hindsight, I wasn't sure if I was strong enough to swing with one arm and shove a flower into a giant's mouth with the other. Damn. Maybe Del had a point.

But we were running out of time, so I called, "I'm ready!"

"Aye, aye." Del pressed her hand against the carving and began to chant, the words a jumble of foreign sounds.

Clarence had said the supernaturals who'd built this place had died out centuries ago. Only a few people knew their odd language, and he'd gotten one to translate a tablet he'd found. Del had an insane memory, so it was her job to memorize the chant and wake the giant.

Del chanted. And chanted.

But nothing happened. Sweat poured down the side of my face as I clung to the vines. Del kept chanting.

"Did Clarence screw us?" I whispered to Nix.

She shrugged, but her gaze was worried.

Suddenly, magic popped and crackled in the air. Awakening. Vines strained as stone shifted. Light shimmered around the giant, highlighting the intricate carving on his crown, which slowly turned from beige to gold. My fingertips tingled. That was a huge crown and a *whole lot* of gold. If I could just snatch it off his head before he turned back to stone, then maybe...

Focus! I fought my dragon covetousness. I didn't even particularly like gold—my idea of treasure was a nice sword or leather jacket—but my dragon side had a real thing for it.

Magic swelled in the air, and the statue of the giant glimmered, his stone body turning to flesh and his massive club becoming wood. His clothing gleamed a rich red in the moonlight, the gold accents glinting under the pale light.

It was working. He was coming alive.

"Who goes there?" His voice rumbled, deep as the pits of hell. He spoke English. He'd been enchanted to speak in the language of whoever was trying to enter, I assumed.

"Now!" Nix whispered.

Go time. I held the flower in one hand and pushed myself off the wall, my other arm straining to hold on. *Oooh, shit.* I gripped the rope with my feet as I swung, praying I wouldn't fall.

I really needed to practice my tomb raiding.

The air whipped by me as I orbited around the giant's head. He shifted to look at me, and my heart thundered. I made eye contact as I reached out for his mouth. Surprise flared in his brown eyes as I shoved the flower at him.

He jerked back, and my fingertips just glanced his lips.

Damn it! I kicked out, attempting to push myself off his chest to try my approach again. If I just swung straight at his face, then maybe...

The giant was having none of it. He reached up with one massive hand and yanked the vine away from the elephant's trunk. He had me dangling like a fish on the line as he swung the vine, sending me flying through the air.

My heart jumped into my throat. I let go just before I would have crashed into one of the massive pillars and grabbed onto a sculpture protruding from the wall. My grip slipped as I tried to cling to the wall and not lose the flower. I dangled, kicking until I found a toehold and managed to claw my way up. I was about level with the giant's head, the flower clutched in my fist.

The giant stood in front of me, about twenty feet to my left. His gaze was pinned on Del and Nix. I made eye contact with my *deirfiúr*, jerking my head to indicate they should try to lead the giant to me.

They sprinted toward me, dodging like they were trying to get around the giant and slip through the entry he guarded. He roared and raised his club, lumbering toward them.

Just as he was about to bring it down on their heads, they darted away, leaping down the stairs toward our motorcycles. The club crashed into the ground, reverberating against the stone tiles.

While he was distracted, I leapt from the wall, aiming for his shoulder. I landed on the back of his neck and clung to his hair.

Gross. It was warm and soft, but way too intimate to be clinging to someone's head.

He swatted back with his hand. I dodged, just barely, and tried to scramble around to the front of his face to shove the flower into his mouth. Maybe we should have baked it into a cake instead.

I'd climbed almost all the way around to his cheek by the time he grabbed me with his big fist. The air whooshed from my lungs as he squeezed, and I swore I felt my ribs grind together. It took all I had to hold onto the flower as he tossed me away. I plummeted and tried to break my fall by rolling, then stumbled to my feet.

"Why have you awoken me?" he bellowed. Rage flared on his face as he swung his head slowly between us.

Nix and Del had climbed the stairs again and now stood in front of him, slightly to either side.

"We're not making a great impression," I hissed at my *deirfiúr*.

"Yeah, I'd say we're not going to convince him to let us in," Del said.

Nix's magic flared, the delicate scent of flowers welling in the air. Light glowed around her hands as she conjured something.

She had a plan. Good. 'Cause I was all out.

The giant stepped forward, toward me.

"Hurry!" I hissed at Nix. I could draw my swords, but he was so damned big.

A second later, a rough rope appeared in Nix's hands. She tossed the other end to Del so that it stretched in front of the giant.

They raced behind him, pulling the rope tight around his legs. He bellowed, then fell, crashing to the stone tiles.

I sprinted for the giant's head, which had hit the ground with a reverberating thunk. Hopefully he was stunned. I dove, skidding on the ground until I was lined up with the giant's face. I shoved the flower into his mouth, trying to keep my arm along his cheek so that he couldn't bite my hand off.

I gagged at the slick feeling of his mouth. He thrashed his head, and I clung like a monkey to the side of his face, my arm buried up to the elbow inside his cheek. It was slimy and horrible, but I wasn't going to give him a chance to spit it out. His thrashing pounded me against the stones.

Finally, he slowed, stilling as the orchid's poison took effect. When I was sure he'd passed out, I released the flower and yanked my hand back, then rolled away.

"Gross, gross, gross!" I shook the spit off my arm as I stood up.

Nix eyed me and said, "Points for commitment."

"Thanks. Good thinking with the rope."

I turned to the passageway that the giant had blocked. It was tall and narrow, a corridor through the massive wall. The moonlight didn't shine far into the tunnel, but there were carvings projecting from the sides that looked like arms reaching out.

I shivered. "Might as well get going. Dawn isn't far off."

"And we don't know how long Mr. Big here will be unconscious," Del said.

I glanced back at the giant, now snoozing peacefully. "Good point. Don't want him chasing after us."

I approached the corridor, waving my hand to ignite the magic in my lightstone ring. The ring flared to life, shining a yellow glow on the passageway.

I led the way through the corridor, weaving between the carvings that reached out toward me. They weren't arms, like I'd thought, but rather vines and roots. I still felt like they were going to grab me.

"These are creepy as hell," Nix whispered.

"No kidding," Del said.

I stepped out on the other side of the tunnel, my eyes widening. Moonlight shined on the massive courtyard spread out in front of me, a sunken pit surrounded on all sides by expansive stairs leading up to the exterior wall. An enormous temple rose up in the middle, its domed, lotus-shaped towers reaching for the moon. It was obviously our destination, but it was the sea of vines that caught my eye.

No, not vines. They were roots from the enormous fig trees that grew up from all the walls, busily consuming this enormous city.

But the roots writhed like snakes.

The giant wasn't the only thing guarding the temple.

"Enchantment, right?" Del said. "Because I don't fancy tangling with real snakes."

"I think so," I said as I drew the swords from my back. I couldn't see any eyes gleaming in the moonlight.

"I don't suppose you could conjure us a jeep or something?" Del asked Nix. "We could plow right through them."

"Sorry, way too complex," Nix said. "Gotta save my strength anyway."

"We'll just hack through it," I said as I stepped forward.

Del drew her sword and joined me. Nix conjured a blade of her own, and we raced down the stairs, taking them two at a time.

I leapt onto the courtyard. The roots shifted under my feet as I ran. One wrapped around my ankle, jerking me to a halt. I fell on my face, pain blasting through my hands.

I pushed myself up. Near my head, there was a root that had been cut in half.

Weird. I was running in front of Del and Nix. Who had cut that root, if not us?

The root gripping my ankle jerked me into the air like a rag doll, scattering my thoughts. Del shrieked. She'd been caught, too, and was now dangling like me. Her dark hair hung down as she strained to reach the root with her blade.

"Hang on!" Nix yelled. She leapt into the air, severing the root that held me. I crashed to the ground as she spun and severed the one that had captured Del.

I scrambled up, Del beside me, and we raced ahead, dodging the grasping roots and swiping others with our blades. I had to cut Nix down once, and by the time we made it to the steps leading up to the main temple, my lungs were burning from the strain and I was covered in scratches.

A massive door was flanked on either side by statues of warriors.

"I sure hope they don't come alive," Nix said.

"Let's not hang around to find out." I pushed the door open, straining against its weight, and slipped into the large entryway.

Del and Nix followed, and I shut the door behind them, hoping to block out any of the more adventurous tree roots from following us.

I raised my hand, shining my lightstone on the space. The walls were elaborately carved, as were the pillars supporting the ceiling.

But something felt off. The air was too fresh. Not stale like most closed-off and forgotten tombs.

"Uh, I thought Clarence said no one had been here in centuries," Del said.

"What?" I glanced at her.

She was pointing at the ground. My eyes followed her fingertip.

Footprints in the dust.

CHAPTER THREE

"Shit," Nix muttered.

"Who the hell would be here?" I asked. "And recently, too, from the looks of it."

"Think they're *still* here?" Nix asked.

"Maybe," I said.

"Another treasure hunter. It's got to be," Del said.

"Yeah, possible." A lot of our jobs for OMB involved breaking into old tombs. We sometimes ran into competition. We were usually quickwitted and skilled enough to get the prize before the other guys, so normally I wouldn't be worried. But this particular prize really mattered. We only had a few hours left before dawn, when OMB turned one of us in.

At that point, our lives were basically over. We were a team. If one of us got nabbed by the Order of the Magica, the others would spend their lives trying to free her. And no one escaped the Order. Trying to escape the Order on top of hiding from the monster who hunted us...

It'd be an impossible situation.

"Let's go," I said. "We need to catch them."

"Agreed," Del said.

"Hang on," Nix said. "What if there are a lot of them? This is a valuable treasure. They might kill to protect it. And doesn't all this feel a little weird? OMB's sudden insistence that we get this treasure. Maybe he knew they were here. So why didn't he warn us?"

Nix was always the cautious one. The one who'd kept us from running headlong into inescapable situations. She wasn't a wimp by any means. In fact, she had the best hand-to-hand skills of any of us. We never killed our competition, unless they were demons, because we were afraid we'd turn into the murderous, power-stealing FireSouls everyone thought our species to be.

But part of not killing our competition was knowing when to bail out. Or at least play it safe.

"You have a point," I said. "OMB wouldn't stop at throwing us into a deadly situation."

"We gotta play by the rules we know," Del said. "Right now, our best odds at continuing another day are to get the daggers for OMB. If we bail now, we'll be on the run from him *and* the Order of the Magica."

"Oh, I'm not suggesting we bail," I said. "We need to keep going. But you be ready to transport us out of here if it gets sticky."

"No problem," Del said.

"Good. As long as we have a plan," Nix said. "Let's get moving."

The grand entry room in which we stood had hallways leading off each of the walls. Massive statues of female warriors wielding clubs stood at either side of each exit. Intricately carved armor covered their chest and thighs. Crowns topped their heads. More Dvarapala. I hoped they didn't come alive.

"Which way?" Del asked.

"I'll check."

I called upon my dragon sense, focusing on what I knew of the daggers to get a link. Del and Nix had the same talent, but mine was strongest. If it was valuable to someone, I could find it. I'd been honing it for the four years we'd worked for OMB.

I envisioned obsidian, the black volcanic glass that the daggers were made of, crafting the image in my head until I felt the familiar tug around my middle, like a rope pulling me toward what I sought.

"Ahead," I said.

We set off across the foyer. I gripped my swords loosely, ready to swing at whatever came my way. Because I couldn't use my magic, what with the fact that I had no control and blew stuff up, I was damned good with weapons.

When we neared the hall we sought, magic swelled in the air. It felt like sticky humidity, even worse than the jungle's normal heat, making my tank top cling to my skin. Fates, I'd give anything to live in a nice, cool climate. We'd been spending too much time in jungle tombs these last four years.

The magic surged, and the stone Dvarapala shifted their clubs sideways, forming an X across the entrance that blocked our path.

"What is your purpose?" The Dvarapala on the left spoke, her voice sounding like stone grinding against stone. Unlike the Dvarapala at the gate entrance, they did not turn to flesh. But they were enchanted to speak our language, as he had been.

"We seek freedom," I said, thinking fast. Honesty was key with situations like these, and word games were common. Because for magic's sake, if you said you were after the treasures they guarded, all hell would break loose.

"Of what kind?" the Dvarapala asked.

"Our own. Freedom from a cruel master." If that wasn't magic's truth, I didn't know what was.

"How will you find it within the temple?" she asked.

"We follow the ones who came before us. We are after them." I held my breath, hoping she'd interpret *after* to mean chasing rather than just literally late to the party.

Her stone lips turned downward. "They are thieves."

So am I. But I tried to look innocent. "We'll stop them from stealing what they seek."

Because we'll steal it first. Obviously, I kept that gem to myself.

"Swear you will abide by that promise, and we will let you pass. Then do with them what you will. But be committed to your goal, because you cannot leave until you complete it."

My shoulders relaxed infinitesimally. She believed we were just after them. I laid a hand over my heart and said, "I swear."

She nodded gravely.

"Hey, real quick," Del said, irreverent as usual. "How'd they get past you?"

I wanted to punch her. We had permission; we just needed to run for it. More conversation meant more ways to reveal our true purpose here, which would definitely end with a fight. These ladies looked faster and smarter than the Dvarapala at the front gate. I didn't want to tangle with them.

"They possess powerful magic," the Dvarapala said. "They froze us in place before we could move. But we cannot leave this hall, so we cannot follow them. But there are more enchantments that could stop them."

"Any tips for getting through?" Del asked.

Damn, she was getting cocky.

"Your worth and skill will see you through. If it does not, then you do not deserve that which you seek."

Fair enough.

The Dvarapala frowned. "Unless you doubt the purity of your purpose here?"

I grabbed Del's arm and squeezed. "We don't. Thank you very much." I bowed low, then tugged Del toward their crossed clubs. The dark hallway beyond beckoned. "Thank you for letting us pass. We will catch them."

The Dvarapala nodded, her gaze sharp on me. Finally, after an interminable few seconds of waiting, she moved her sword, and her partner did the same.

The path was clear.

I held my breath as we hurried through, raising my lightstone ring to illuminate the intricately carved tile corridor with pillars on either side. When we were far enough away that I could no longer feel the sticky humidity of the Dvarapala's magic, my shoulders relaxed.

"You really press our luck, you know that?" I said to Del.

"Yep. But now we know there are more challenges ahead. And that our competition has powerful magic."

"Yeah, that's not great news," I said.

"But it is good to know," Nix said from behind.

"True." I had to give them that one. "Just keep an eye out."

We followed the corridor for several minutes, trying to keep our footsteps soft on the tile. The walls were covered in detailed carvings of people and animals, telling some kind of story I couldn't decipher.

"Feels like they're watching us," I said.

"Yeah, there was a monkey carving back there giving me the evil eye," Del said.

"Are we going downhill?" Nix asked. "It's getting cooler. And I think there's a slope to the ground."

I turned my head to look behind us as I walked, trying to tell if the ground sloped up. I squinted, tilting my head each way. "I can't—"

My next step met nothing but air. The ground disappeared from under me. I screamed as I fell, clawing at the air. Something latched onto the sword harness that crisscrossed over my back, jerking me to a halt. I dangled like a yo-yo over a pit.

I looked up. Del lay on her stomach, her arm stretched down, clutching the back of my sword harness. Nix scrambled down next to her and reached for my hand. I clasped hers, trying my damnedest to spin and get a foothold on the side of the pit.

"You gotta watch where you're going," Del bit out. Her face twisted with the effort of holding onto me.

I caught a toehold on the rough stone wall and pushed, helping them pull me out of the pit.

"You guys are the best," I panted as I scrambled onto the tile floor. "What the hell happened?"

"You were looking behind you, dummy." Del shoved her hair off her face. "And there's a booby trap full of giant spiders blocking the path. The pit was covered by an illusion, but there was a sheen of magic I could see. I spotted it right as your foot went in."

I swear I could feel the blood drain from my face. "Spiders?"

"Yeah, your fave," Nix said.

I grimaced and leaned over to look into the pit. The bottom was only about twenty feet away, but it was just a black, writhing mass of enormous spiders.

"Nope, nope, nope." I crawled back from the ledge. The corridor continued on the other side of the pit, which was about ten feet wide. Too far to jump. "There should be a secret lever of some kind that'll make a bridge or something to help us cross. But we don't have a ton of time to figure it out."

I didn't actually know that for a fact, but that was how it usually worked.

"Let me see what I can do," Nix said.

Her magic swelled in the air, the floral scent driving away the smell of damp stone that permeated the temple. A narrow wooden bridge appeared over the pit.

"Thanks," I said as I climbed to my feet.

My heart jumped into my throat as I stepped up to the edge of the skinny bridge. It was only about a foot wide and wobbly, but I didn't want to ask Del to expend any more magical energy. She should save it for our confrontation with whoever was ahead of us.

"Watch where you're going," Del said. "Eyes forward."

I laughed weakly and swallowed bile at the thought of walking over the spiders on this glorified popsicle stick. I would definitely be paying attention from now on.

"Here goes nothing." I hurried across, then turned back and gave the thumbs up.

Nix and Del followed, one at a time, then we hurried down the corridor. I held my lightstone ring aloft and kept my attention glued ahead of me, senses on high alert for the feeling of magic that might save me from another fall.

We came to several crossroads and passed through a few empty rooms, but my dragon sense kept pulling me forward.

"We're definitely sloping downward," Nix said.

"Yeah." But I didn't look back to confirm.

The smell of smoke made my nose twitch. It was the only warning I got.

"Back!" I shouted, then spun and threw myself in the other direction, pushing Nix and Del out of harm's way.

Warm orange light illuminated the corridor. I spun back to see what magic had ignited. A wall of flame crackled in front of us, bright orange and yellow and blocking the way entirely.

"Shit," Nix said. "That makes up for missing the spider hole. How'd you sense it?"

"Smelled smoke right before it burst to life."

"I can try transporting us to the other side," Del said.

"Might as well try," I said.

Transporting was usually magically barred in places like this; otherwise there'd be no point in putting all the booby traps in place. Transporting out was usually possible, but even that wasn't guaranteed.

Del reached for my hand, and I grasped it. Nix did the same. The fresh laundry scent of Del's magic surged on the air, but we didn't go anywhere.

Del opened her eyes. "Nothing."

"Let's try this, then," Nix said. I smelled the floral scent of her magic, then three fire extinguishers appeared before her.

"Good idea." I reached for one.

"Maybe," she said. "Just be quick. That fire is burning magic, not wood, so we can't put it out. We can just minimize it long enough to get through."

"I'll go first." I fiddled with the fire extinguisher, jumping when it blasted a cloud of white in front of me. "Jeeze."

Someone coughed. The haze of white dust dissipated.

Del stared back at me, her face white with powder. "Just point it at the fire, genius."

I laughed—I couldn't help it, I was a jerk—then turned to face the fire. I got close enough that I could feel the heat on my face, then blasted the ground right in front of me. The fire disappeared for a second, then came back.

Okay. So I'd have to be *really* quick. I sprayed the fire, focusing on a thin vertical strip about as tall and wide as me.

"Go!" Del shouted. "It's big enough!"

I sprinted through the gap, the flame on either side singeing the hair on my arms. Pain flared, but at least I didn't smell burning flesh. The corridor looked the same as it had on the other side of the flame.

"It's fine over here!" I called.

Del and Nix sprinted through a moment later, their hair singed at the ends and their eyes wild.

Nix coughed as she said, "Not a fan of that."

"I should be able to transport us out," Del said. "So we only have to do that once."

"Thank magic for that." I put my fire extinguisher near the wall and continued down the corridor, holding my lightstone ring aloft.

It was too bad Nix couldn't make things disappear in the same way she made them appear. Leaving the fire extinguishers behind felt like littering on a historic site.

"Oh, shit, do you smell that?" Nix said as we neared the end of the corridor. The space beyond was black.

"Ugh, yeah." I waved my hand in front of my face. "Smells like animal, or something."

"I'd get your swords out," Del said.

I was already drawing mine. I didn't like killing animals—like, really didn't like it, went to extreme measures to not kill even the demon hounds that guarded tombs—but I had to at least be prepared to protect us. I couldn't conjure and I couldn't transport, but stabbing things was well within my skill set.

I just hoped I wouldn't have to stab anything with a fluffy tail. Demon hounds might have puppy dog eyes, but they also had eight-inch fangs, acid saliva, and a thirst for blood that rivaled a vampire's. I actually quite liked them.

We approached the blackness at the end of the tunnel in a fanned out V-shape. Del and Nix walked at my sides, armed with their own swords. My lightstone ring lit the way.

When we stepped out of the tunnel, our footsteps echoed. The room was so big that the light from my ring didn't reach the edges. I blinked, confused at what I was seeing.

There were balls scattered all over the floor, about the size of basketballs.

"Shiiit," Del breathed.

Something glinted on one of the balls. I stutter-stepped.

They weren't balls. They were heads. Snake heads.

The animal smell wasn't demon hounds. It was a snake's den.

I thrust my arm out, trying to cast as much light as possible into the cavern. Shadows stretched from all ends, shrouding the room in creepiness.

A massive, seven-headed snake guarded a door at the other end. Its heads—all freaking seven of them—whipped toward us, alerted by my light, no doubt.

The snake surged forward, its huge body graceful and quick

on the stones. The sound of its belly slithering along the floor, knocking aside heads, made me shudder.

"It's a Naga. Chop off its heads!" Del said. "That'll incapacitate it long enough for us to get past."

Incapacitate, but not kill. The heads on the ground had once belonged to this snake. Whoever had come before us had chopped them all off, and it had grown them right back.

At least I wouldn't have to kill it.

The snake was still a dozen yards away when one of the heads reared back and spat a neon green fluid at us. It glittered in the light of my ring. I dived to the side, barely missing being splattered. When it hit the ground, the stone floor sizzled.

My favorite. Venom-spitting, seven-headed snakes.

"Retreat!" I called. "Let's find another way in."

"Seconded!" Del shouted as she spun to head back down the corridor.

But there was no more corridor. There was nothing but a smooth expanse of stone.

"Shit!" Del shouted. "We're trapped!"

Damn it!

What had the female Dvarapala said? Be committed to your goal because you cannot leave until you complete it, or something?

Just perfect. This job was getting stickier and stickier as it went.

I spun back to face the Naga. "Del! Give me a toss."

"On it!" She ran to my side.

"Take this!" Nix shouted. Her magic flared, and she threw a small shield at me.

I shoved one of my blades into its sheath and caught the shield, then charged the Naga, Del racing slightly ahead of me. My heart pounded so hard I thought it would break my ribs, but the only way to deal with problems as big as this was to run at them.

Literally, in this case.

The Naga loomed fifteen feet above us, too tall for me to reach on my own. Del still ran five feet ahead of me. When we were close enough to see its fangs glinting, Del skidded to one knee, cupping her hands. I sprinted toward her, putting one foot into her cupped palms. She pushed up as I launched myself off her hands and into the air, slicing my blade toward the Naga's closest head.

My sword went clean through, severing the first head. I followed through and took off a second, then grabbed onto one of the necks with my shielded arm, clinging like a monkey and swiping out with my blade. Another head fell as the snake struck out, its head coming straight for me.

I shrunk back, hiding behind the neck I clung to and raising my shield. Vibrations sang up my arm when its head collided with the metal, but I ignored it and reached around, slicing off the now-stunned head with my blade.

Four down, three to go.

I looked up at the head attached to the neck to which I clung. An arrow thudded into its eye. Nix with a conjured bow and arrow, I assumed. The other two heads received arrows in short order, and I sliced them all off.

The snake's massive body collapsed when its last head toppled to the ground. I leapt away, not wanting to spend the next hour trapped beneath a giant snake, only to be released when it woke up and moved.

"Good work," Del said.

"Thanks for the boost." I set off toward the exit, Nix and Del at my side. I sure as hell didn't want to be around the Naga when it woke again, but I kept my grip on the shield just in case. Nix held on to her bow, the quiver still strapped over her back.

I halted when I reached the exit, now rightly wary. My heart would probably burst right now if I fell into a pit of spiders. I thrust out my hand, letting my lightstone ring illuminate the corridor. It was short, leading to a big door.

"Looks safe enough," I said.

"That's relative, but I'm cool with it," Del said.

I grinned and stepped into the corridor. At the end, we pushed open the door and found a wide set of stairs leading down.

"All the good shit is always underground," Nix said.

She hated it underground, but I didn't mind so much. I led the way, keeping my steps quiet.

"Smells fresh," Del said. "Kinda like water."

"Maybe we're close." I stopped at the landing at the bottom of the stairs. About twenty feet ahead of us was a massive set of golden doors. In front of them stood a Dvarapala, his head almost brushing the ceiling. He was twice as massive as the one who'd guarded the front gate. Thirty feet tall if he was an inch. And I was out of sleeping potion flowers.

I stepped forward. Magic swirled around him, bringing with it the scent of wet stone. He came alive, his stone turning to flesh and his weapons to metal. His gaze narrowed on us.

"What do you offer?" His voice was deep and scratchy.

"Tribute," Del whispered. "Payment to enter. We've made it this far, so he assumes we're legit."

"Um..."

"Your swords," he rumbled.

My grip tightened on my sword. The other was sheathed at my back, but I wanted to grab that one too. I liked these blades. I'd saved up for over a year to get my hands on them.

"I can conjure better blades," Nix said to him. "Any kind you like."

I shot her a grateful glance.

"Those blades." The Dvarapala pointed. "They are of value. I see how she cherishes them. Tribute must be of value."

I forced myself to loosen my grip on my blade. He was right.

We couldn't trick him. If he had anything like my dragon sense, he could tell what was valuable and what wasn't.

"It's fine." I stepped forward and held out my swords.

"You love those," Nix hissed.

"We need to get through. And look at him." I nodded at his set face. "He's determined. And thirty feet tall."

"Yeah." Nix's voice was low.

We approached and I laid the blades at his feet, something in my chest tightening when I stood.

The Dvarapala nodded and stepped aside. Together, we leaned against one of the massive doors, slowly pushing it open.

The sight of the mountains of glittering gold hit me in the chest. Small balls of flame hovered in the air, shining golden light onto the coins, statues, jewelry, and crowns that were piled all around. Gems littered the space as well. So much so that it was almost like a cartoon. The huge room was filled to the brim, like Scrooge McDuck's swimming pool full of gold coins. Through the middle ran a glittering blue river.

I couldn't even think about the oddness of an underground river as covetousness surged within me. I wanted to shove my pockets full of the shining stuff. Stick one of the many crowns on my head. I stepped in, dazed. Nix and Del followed, no doubt as riveted as I was. The door slammed shut behind us.

We walked into the room like zombies, our gazes glued to all the shiny, yellow metal. We all had different opinions about what real treasure was, but we couldn't escape our dragon's love for gold.

"We need to find the daggers," Del murmured.

I nodded, my eyes on a massive golden Buddha. Whatever supernaturals had built this place, they'd been seriously into the gold.

The river burbled to my left, flowing swiftly downstream and out through a tunnel at the other side of the room. Gold glittered at the bottom, as if some of the piles of coins had just slid in the water and stayed there.

On the whole, I didn't like stealing from ancient temples. I only did it because OMB would ruin my life if I didn't. But being surround by this much wealth—enough to buy our way free a dozen times over—I couldn't help but try to rationalize it.

I wandered away from the river, toward the biggest piles. Del and Nix did the same, drawn as I was to the shining towers.

"About time you got here," a voice said.

My heart thumped. I spun around. OMB stood in front of the river, his malevolent gaze latched on us.

CHAPTER FOUR

Shock jerked me out of my trance. I shook away the gold stupor, annoyed at my weakness. Sometimes, my FireSoul got the better of me.

"What the hell are you doing here?" I raked my gaze over the old asshole who'd made our lives hell for the last four years.

He looked like some Jimmy-Buffet-Margaritaville wannabe with his white beard and Hawaiian shirt. But not cheerful. Horrible and creepy. His magic tasted like dirt. My skin crawled just from looking at him. We only saw him a few times a year and tried to keep it like that for this very reason.

Another man stepped out from behind a different pile of gold. Big and broad shouldered, he looked like a linebacker but dressed like an accountant. Six demons appeared at his side, melting out of the shadows. Their skin was the dusky red of some kind of fire demon. They must have created the fire balls that illuminated the room. And there'd be more where that came from.

Just what we needed. My heart thundered, echoing in my ears.

But it was the sight of the metal shackles dangling from the linebacker's hand that made my skin really crawl. I glanced behind us, unsurprised to see that the doors had disappeared.

Just like the female Dvarapala had said. Complete your goal if you want to get out.

Del grabbed my hand. I felt her magic swell as she tried to teleport us out of here. I approved. This was a trap, and the odds were against us.

But nothing happened.

"Do you really think you can just teleport out of here?" OMB asked snidely.

"Obviously, I'd hoped so," Del said. "Because whatever this sausage-fest is, I don't want to be part of it."

I silently applauded her bitchiness. We were never rude to OMB—we were too scared of him—but once a guy had trapped you in a room with two dudes, six demons, and a handful of shackles, there was no talking your way out of it. His intentions were bad.

"Oh, but we've set this up for you," OMB said.

"Clearly," I spat. Whatever he wanted from us, he'd had to get us into a room we couldn't escape, not even with Del's teleporting. "Are there any daggers, or was this just your attempt to trap us?"

"Both." He reached into the pocket of his stupid, baggy linen pants and tugged out two obsidian daggers. He tossed one into the air, and it flipped end over end, black glass glittering in the light. "These are quite nice, actually."

My eyes followed it, true covetousness welling in me. Not the semi-false kind that came from my FireSoul's love for gold, but my own desire. I liked weapons—no, I *loved* weapons—and those were beautiful.

OMB caught the dagger. "I'm selling you. Arturo here has offered me an excellent price."

"Selling us?" I shrieked, finally forgetting the fear that had kept me polite all these years. "You can't sell us! You don't freaking *own* us."

"Of course I do. What do you think blackmail is?"

"Uh, it doesn't involve shackles." I could smell the floral scent of Nix's magic as she worked to subtly conjure something. Whatever it was, I wanted to give her time to finish.

"Either way, you're my most valuable asset. And I'm done using you for petty thievery."

Petty? We'd stolen millions of dollars worth of stuff for him.

"I'm going to sell you for one lump sum and not have to worry about you anymore. You were easier and more malleable when you were younger. Now that you're adults and you've been talking about buying you're freedom... It's just easier to sell you." He smiled and the hair on my arms stood up. "I'd have liked to have made the transfer in an easier way, but I had a feeling you wouldn't be amenable to it in the first place."

"Amenable? You're selling our freedom! To a guy with shackles!"

"Freedom?" He scoffed. "You've never had freedom. Just the illusion of it. But Arturo isn't interested in the illusion."

Holy shit, this was bad. Our worst-case-scenario for this job had been a scuffle with some other treasure hunters. This was nightmarish in comparison.

I eyed the shackles. "I can't exactly hunt treasure if I'm bound in chains."

Come on, Nix. Hurry. I hoped she was conjuring a grenade launcher, even though I knew that was outside of her capabilities. I eyed a sword sticking out of a pile of gold to my left. If she wasn't conjuring weapons, I'd need it.

"Oh, that's not what I want you for," Arturo said. His voice had the smooth accent of an upper class Brit. "I run a supernatural fight ring. You will be the highlight of my empire. Fight to the death, kill, and steal the powers of your opponents."

Horror made my brain go blank. I'd thought there was only

one way to exploit a FireSoul—be like OMB and force us to find treasure. This was more awful than I could even imagine.

"Think of the crowds. There to watch FireSouls in their natural habitat." He grinned wide.

My mouth opened and shut, no words coming out. Arturo's eyes gleamed with excitement and a bit of madness. It was the most insane, terrible, cocky idea I'd ever heard. We'd be exposed to hundreds of supernaturals, eventually the Order of the Magica —because there was no way this could run unnoticed—and be forced to kill?

Hell no. On so many levels.

I forced myself to find my voice and take advantage of Arturo's hubris. Fear and anger were the only things I could feel, so it took all I had to lace my voice with derision. "If you make us so powerful with all the stolen powers, how exactly are you going to control us?" I tsk-tsked. "You've really got to think these things through."

"We have our ways." His voice was so cold, so ominous, that I shivered, my false bravado deflated. I believed him. There were many, many ways to control people. Even powerful FireSouls.

Behind the men and the demons, a small boat appeared out of nowhere, floating on the river near the exit, where the water flowed out through a tunnel.

Nix had conjured an escape route for us. I didn't know where that river led, but it was better than here. We just had to get there.

We could go through our enemy or around them, weaving our way between the piles of gold until we reached the little boat.

I lunged for the sword to my left, yanking it out of the pile of gold. Nix raised her bow and arrow and fired, hitting the demon to Arturo's right. He collapsed.

His brethren raised their hands and threw fireballs at us. They streaked through the air as we dived behind a pile of gold. Coins flew as the fire hurtled into the pile.

"We gotta get those daggers," I said. "Or the temple won't let us escape."

"And kill OMB," Del said.

"And Arturo. They know what we are," Nix said. Her magic flared as she conjured shields and handed one off to Del.

"Agreed." I hadn't wanted to kill before this. Now, I had no problem with it. These bastards deserved to die. I just didn't know how we would accomplish it. OMB had the gift of psychometry, allowing him to understand an object's history. He'd be easy prey, but I didn't know what Arturo's magical gift was. And those demons would make this tough.

"You two block me and I'll shoot," Nix said.

The pile of gold behind us exploded. We flew forward, heat from the fireballs searing our backs.

Go time.

We scrambled to our feet, Del and I clutching our shields. We knelt in front of Nix, shields raised to protect her. Over the top, Nix fired three arrows in lightning-fast succession. She'd always been the best shot.

Arturo raised a hand, knocking them out of the air.

"Shit!" He was telekinetic.

My shield jerked. He was trying to take it! I gripped it tighter.

"Back," I said. "This won't work."

We raced behind the next pile of gold, eyeing our escape route. OMB stood slightly away from Arturo and his demons. We just had to get to him, then beyond to the boat. We could hunt Arturo later.

"You've gotta try your magic, Cass," Del said.

I glanced at her, shocked. The few times I'd used it, I'd lost control and caused explosions.

But then, that was exactly what we needed right now. If I couldn't master the fire demon's flame, I could at least cause a distraction. And this place was stone. I couldn't burn it to the ground, at least.

"Yeah, okay, I—"

The pile of gold behind us blew apart as fireballs slammed into it. Again, we were thrown to the ground, skidding on the stone floor.

"Your shield!" Nix said.

I handed her my shield, and we all crouched, Nix and Del protecting me from the fireballs that plowed at us. I reached for my magic, calling it up from deep inside me. It was hard to get a grip on something that I'd kept locked up for so long, but I pushed through. My magic flared to life, an electric energy in my chest, roaring to be released.

It took everything I had to suppress it as I searched for the fire demon's signature. I had to identify it and command the flame. Take it for my own. The burn of smoke filled my nose as my magic latched on to it. My mind filled with images of a giant fireball enveloping the demons and Arturo.

The fire magic burned beneath my skin, raring to be released. I pushed my hands between Nix and Del and the shields they held, releasing the burning magic that filled my body.

Enormous balls of fire formed and floated overhead, and a huge jet of smoke shot through the air. It bowled over the demons and Arturo, then plowed into a pile of gold on the other side of the river. Two of the demons plunged into the water.

More smoke began to fill the room, mushroom clouds of it forming and expanding. It was far from the controlled jet of fire I'd been hoping for, but it'd do.

"Go!" I shouted as the air turned smoky and opaque.

The demons were rising, their hands glowing orange as they charged up with fireballs. Arturo surged to his feet and waved his hands, his face alight with rage.

Massive piles of gold coins swept into the air and flew through the room like crazed bees, hordes of them swooping and zooming around. One crashed into another pile of treasure, sending the gold flying.

Hoping the smoke would hide us, we raced toward where OMB had been standing, dodging the coins and fire as my smoke made it almost impossible to see. Our magic was no match for Arturo's, but killing OMB was still possible if we could find him in the smoke. And we had to get those daggers if we wanted to escape, since they were our original purpose for being here.

A choked scream sounded to my left. I glanced over in time to see Del crash to the ground as a horde of coins bowled her over. Nix skidded over to try to pull her up.

I spun to help, but Nix yelled, "I've got her. Get the daggers!"

I nodded and turned, racing toward OMB. My eyes burned from the smoke, and I could barely make out his bright Hawaiian shirt. But he was on the ground, not standing. I'd psyched myself up for killing him—I no longer had a problem with that, given what he'd done—but as I landed on my knees near his body, I realized I wouldn't have to.

His head was on fire, and he lay still as death. As I watched, the flame ignited his horrible shirt.

Dead. By my magic or a stray fireball from the demons, I didn't know.

I didn't care.

Near his body, the daggers lay on the stone where he'd dropped them. I snatched them up and surged to my feet. My *deirfiúr* appeared at my side a moment later, Nix supporting Del.

I could see nothing but smoke surrounding us, though I could hear the flying coins crashing into things. My magic had gone out of control, and Arturo appeared to have taken the Destroy Everything method of defeating an enemy. I couldn't even see the river.

I focused on my dragon sense, searching for the boat. The familiar tug about my middle directed me left.

I wrapped my arm around Del's waist. "Come on, this way."

We headed toward the boat as fast as we could, Del improving with every step.

Something massive and hard plowed into my back, knocking me flat on my face. I dragged myself up, clawing my way out from beneath a pile of coins. Nix and Del dragged me free, and we limped toward the boat.

When it appeared through the smoke, I grinned, grateful that it hadn't been destroyed.

We leapt inside and pushed off the wall, catching the current. Fresh air whooshed over us as we floated through the dark tunnel. I slumped on the seat, aches and pains all over. Those coins packed a hell of a punch. I shoved the daggers into my tall boots, hoping they wouldn't nick me.

"Holy shit, we made it," Del said.

"Almost," I said, squinting into the dark. How far had we drifted?

"Your light, Cass," Nix said.

"One sec." I wanted to make sure we were far enough away from the tunnel entrance that Arturo couldn't see the glow through the smoke. I wasn't sure if he'd seen the boat, but I wanted to play it safe.

A few moments later, I raised my hand, allowing the light-stone ring to glow. The tunnel was roughly carved out of rock. The water glittered blue in the light.

"I'll transport us out of here whenever I get my power back," Del said. "I don't know how long the temple will block it."

"Maybe the river will run out of the temple." I grabbed the oars that lay in the bottom of the boat and began to row. Whatever was at the other end, I wanted to reach it quickly.

"You feeling okay, Del?"

"Yeah. Just bruised."

"We're going to have to find Arturo," Nix said. "And kill him. Soon. Before he can tell anyone what we are."

"Yeah." I'd never hunted a man with the intent to kill him before, but there was no way around this. It had to happen. Even if we managed to buy the concealment charms we wanted, they couldn't hide us if Arturo told the world what we were. There was nothing strong enough to protect us from that.

"Up ahead," Del said.

I stopped rowing and turned. The tunnel opened to a wider space. Light flowed in from the top.

"A sinkhole," Nix said.

I rowed harder, desperate to get away from this damned temple. We floated into the enormous cavern. Sunlight shined down through the small hole about twenty feet above, and vines dangled down.

"Can you transport us, Del?" I asked.

She shook her head. "Still blocked."

"So we're still inside the temple walls," Nix said.

"Probably." I lined us up beneath the hole in the ground and looked up. The vines dangled down far enough that we could reach if we stood up.

"Looks like we're climbing," Del said.

"Yep." I stood.

The boat wobbled, but we each managed to grab a thick vine and began to climb. My arms burned as I made my way up. By the time I grabbed on to the rock lining the edge of the hole, I wasn't sure I could've climbed another foot.

I scrambled onto the jungle floor and stood. Stone statues surrounded us on all sides, like a protective circle. About a hundred yards away, the tall outer walls of the temple compound rose high. We were still inside.

"Hurry," I said. "Let's get out of here."

We hurried to the edge of the stone circle. As soon as I passed between two of the stones, something hit me in the head. Pain flared and blackness followed.

CHAPTER FIVE

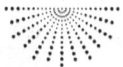

Pain stabbed me in the head, and pressure pounded my aching middle. I opened my eyes, confused to see the floor bouncing beneath me. My arms hung down, shackled.

My heartbeat deafened me as I glanced around, trying to get my bearings without moving. I was slung over the shoulder of one of the fire demons, being carried down a hallway. We were alone in the hall. Heavy metal doors passed by, dotting the stone corridor.

Shit. Cells.

For a second, I was terrified that the Order of the Magica had captured us. But this was a fire demon carrying me.

It had to have been Arturo. We were probably at his fighting compound, or wherever he kept the fighters locked up.

My mind raced. I had to get out of this. Find Nix and Del. I could try to create another smoke cloud by mirroring the fire demon's magic, but I was just as likely to light us both up in this small space as I was to make smoke.

And the gross, empty feeling filling in my middle meant these shackles were repressing my magic. So even if I wanted to, I didn't think I could magic my way out of this.

I clutched my hands together, pressing the iron cuffs against each other. They were massively heavy, a weapon in their own right. I swung my arms hard, nailing the demon in the kidney. At least, I assumed his kidney was there since he was human-shaped.

He grunted in pain and doubled over. I flailed, shifting just enough to bring my shackles down on the back of his head. He stumbled to his knees, dropping me.

I scrambled back.

He recovered quickly, his face twisting in anger as he reached for me. But he was slow, no doubt seeing double from my blow to the back of his head. I kicked out, deflecting one of his hands and rolling to the side. My daggers were no longer shoved in my boot, or I'd have used them.

Before he could call on his fire, I scrambled behind him and jumped on his back, wrapping the chain connecting the shackles around his neck.

I pulled hard and demanded, "Where are we?"

He grunted.

I loosened the shackles to hear his response, but he used the reprieve to reach around and grab the back of my shirt. With an enormous heave, he threw me off him. I flew through the air and skidded against the stone. Pain flared in my shoulder where I hit the ground. I pushed it aside and scrambled up.

My gaze caught on gleaming black glass stuck into his belt. The daggers.

I lunged for them, managed to grab one. The demon grabbed my hair and tugged me upright. I plunged the blade into his chest. His eyes widened.

Had the idiot thought I wouldn't go for the blades? Or had he forgotten they were there because they were so new?

I didn't care. I just twisted the blade, then raised a knee and kicked off him. He stumbled onto his back. I surged to my feet and leapt onto him, straddling his chest and plunging the dagger again.

Warm blood welled. His eyes closed.

Dead.

I left the dagger in his chest and patted down his pockets, searching for a key to the shackles.

Come on, come on.

Empty. Damn it.

I yanked the dagger from his chest and wiped the blood on his shirt, then tucked the blade into my boot. I tugged the other knife from his belt and stood, surveying my surroundings. The hall extended about fifty meters in each direction, metal cell doors leading off all sides.

Nix and Del could be in any of these. I focused on my dragon sense, picturing my *deirfiúr* and calling upon my desire to find them. The familiar tug about my middle pulled immediately, directing me back toward the direction the demon had been coming from. Perhaps he'd dropped my sisters off first.

I spared one last glance for the body of the demon, hoping he'd disappear soon. That was the one convenient thing about demons—give them a few minutes, and their bodies returned to their hell. No cleanup needed. If he disappeared before any of his kin found him, they might think I was locked away in whatever miserable cell they'd planned to put me in.

My dragon sense led me down the hall almost to the end. The second to last door on the right beckoned. I reached it and knocked softly on the metal, peering through the tiny glass window.

"Nix? Del?" I called in a low voice.

"Cass!" Nix's face popped up in the tiny window. "Where's Del?"

"You don't have her?"

"No. Arturo's goons took her."

"Shit." My mind raced.

"Hey! What's going on out there?" a feminine voice called from the cell next to Nix's.

I ran to the door and peeked in. A pretty, dark-haired girl stared back. She was about my age, but her eyes made her look older. I wondered how long she'd been in here.

"What's happening?" Her accent was British.

I spoke in a low voice. "Prison break. I'll get you out if you shut up. Don't alert the guards."

"Fine. You have a key?"

"No, but I'll find one."

"Most guards carry keys. Their quarters are on the other side of the fight hall. I've heard they eat at noon in the mess hall, so their quarters should be emptier. Just a couple of the night shift guys sleeping. Assuming they sleep. You'll only have one to fight for a key. Two at most."

I was right. She had been here a while. Long enough to know the guards, at least. I called upon my dragon sense to confirm her words, focusing on the key I sought.

The tug about my waist pulled me in multiple directions. One was strongest, and I figured that was where most of the guards were having lunch. There were more keys there, but more guards. So that was a no-go. The lighter tug pulled down the hall and farther away, into another part of the building.

That must be what she'd told me about. The quarters.

"Hey, you there?" she asked.

I glanced at her. "Sorry. And yeah, I'll find the key and come back for you."

"I'm Claire," she said. "Don't forget me."

"I won't." I went back to Nix's cell. "I'm getting a key. I'll come back and spring you, then we'll get Del back."

"Be safe," Nix called.

"My middle name," I said.

Her wry laugh echoed through the door.

I raced down the hall, the dagger clutched in my hand, ready to throw if necessary. When I reached the heavy metal door at the end, I pressed myself against the wall, then slowly pried the door open.

A figure stood in the small room, his back to me. He wore a dark blue guard's uniform. He spun, but I was quicker, throwing the dagger. The black glass sank into his neck. His eyes widened and he collapsed, blood dripping from his lips as he gasped.

His skin was a dull gray. Another demon.

I fell on him, searching his pockets for keys. Nothing, again. Would have been too good to be true. But I found a handkerchief.

The sound of a roaring crowd sounded through the heavy door on the other side of the room.

The fight ring.

I pulled the handkerchief out, yanked the blade from his chest, then awkwardly draped the cloth over my bound wrists. It was an awful disguise, but at least it wasn't noticeable at first glance that I was cuffed. I hoped the crowd in the fight ring would be thick enough that I could get lost in them.

I ran to the door, but stopped short so that I could walk through like I owned the place.

This was insane.

There could be a guard on the other side. Someone could see me.

But it was also the only way to save Del and Nix. There'd been no exit at the other end of the hall, so there was no roundabout way to get to the key that didn't involve going through the guard.

I pulled the door open and strode through. Immediately, I was bombarded by sound and darkness. Colored lights cut through the gloom, illuminating a massive crowd and a huge demon standing in front of me. He turned, and I recognized the dark blue guard's uniform. For a split second, his confused gaze darted to my white, cloth-covered hands, then he reached for his weapon. I struck, plunging the blade into his chest.

His knees weakened immediately, but I plunged the blade

deeper, straining to hold him upright. We were against a wall, with the crowd facing the fight ring in the middle of the room, but it would look weird if he immediately collapsed.

Slowly, I let him slide to the floor, my attention sharp on the crowd behind him. It didn't look like anyone noticed us. By the time I got him on the ground, he was dead. I patted down his pockets just to make sure there were no keys, then looked up.

A boy towered over me, his dark hair flopping over his forehead and his band t-shirt making him look young. He couldn't be more than seventeen, and he was no guard.

"What the hell are you doing?" he demanded in a thick British accent.

"Uh." Normally I'd throw a dagger at this point, but no way was I gonna kill some idiot kid who was at a fight club for some thrills.

"You came from the cells," he said.

"No, I didn't."

"You're wearing shackles, so you did. Did you see my sister?"

"Sister?" I stood.

"Yeah. She's in there. Are you escaping?"

"Come on, kid." I grabbed his arm and dragged him away from the demon, keeping his body between me and the crowd, using him to hide my shackles as we made our way around the perimeter to the guard's quarters on the other side. "You're after your sister, huh?"

"Yeah. She was snatched and taken here. Her name's Claire. I'm doing some recon to save her."

Recon to save her? At least the kid had heart, though I doubted his odds of success. He was skinny and young. His magic smelled like baking bread and cinnamon. No way this kid was a fighter.

"It's your lucky day, kid. We're going to rescue my sisters and yours, too. Now stay between me and the crowd so no one sees my shackles."

The place was heaving, with hundreds of bodies standing and cheering around a caged fight ring in the center. Two shifters. A wolf and a bear, going at it under threat of death.

"All right." He tried to puff himself up, which actually worked a little since he was so tall. "What's our plan?"

"Break into the guards' quarters, steal a key, and let them out."

"That's it?"

"I haven't had a lot of time to plan." I glanced up at him. "You with me? 'Cause I'm your best shot."

"Yeah, I'm with you."

"Good. Guards' quarters are on the other side of the ring."

We stuck to the wall, pushing our way through the crowd at the back and veering around any demons we saw. I couldn't be sure they were guards, but I didn't want to find out.

"I think it's that door." The kid pointed to a plain metal one. "I've seen a lot of guards come and go through there. A whole bunch just left a while ago."

Going to lunch, if Claire was right.

"Good," I said. "You're not too bad at recon. Can you fight?"

"Yeah."

"With magic?"

"Just potion bombs. I'm a Hearth Witch."

As I'd thought. "Bring any?"

He patted the pocket of his jacket. "A few. Fire and death acid."

"Good. Don't hesitate to use them. We're sneaking in and jumping the first guard with a key, then heading back to the cells." I'd use my dragon sense to figure out which guard had a key. Hopefully we could avoid any unnecessary fights.

He nodded.

I leaned myself up against his side and said, "Put your arm around me. Pretend like you're supporting a drunk person. If we see a guard, we'll try to play it off. If he has a key, I'll tell you. Then we attack."

"All right."

I focused on my dragon sense, grateful for the immediate tug around my middle. There was a key nearby.

"Now?" the kid asked.

"Yeah."

He pushed open the door, and I stumbled through, putting some of my weight on him and tucking my handkerchief-covered hands close to his side to hide them.

We walked into another hall, this one with open doors along it. The first room we passed was a rec room with a TV and couch. The second was an empty bedroom. The third had a closed door, but my dragon sense pulled me hardest toward whatever was within.

If I had to bet, the demon inside was sleeping. We were going to ambush him, and it was going to be gruesome as hell, probably. Normally, I wouldn't sneak up on someone like this.

But with my *deirfiúr* at risk?

I could set my standards aside. I pulled away from the kid and looked up at him, whispering, "Get your bombs."

He pulled two glass vials out of his pockets. One was red, one green. Fire and acid. I didn't need the acid destroying the key, and I didn't want to search a body that was on fire. I also didn't want this kid to have to commit murder with me.

"Stay here," I whispered. "Throw those if anyone comes at us."

He nodded and turned to face the hall, guarding me. I tossed the handkerchief aside and raised my knife, then nudged open the door.

As I'd thought, the demon was lying on his back, dead asleep. I stepped across the threshold, quiet as I could, but a buzzing alarm broke the silence.

The demon jerked awake, bolting upright and grabbing the stun gun at his thigh. I threw my knife, pinning his hand to the bed. He dropped the stun gun and growled. His gaze met mine as I reached down to pull the other knife from my boot. Hampered by my cuffs, I fumbled it and cut my finger on the blade, but I managed to pull it out.

The dagger in his hand jerked itself free and flew back through the air, headed straight for me. Panicked, I flung my blade at him and caught the one flying at me.

Ohh, so that's how they work. My blood must have ignited the spell that allowed the enchanted daggers to return to their owner. Cool.

The knife I'd thrown thudded into the demon's shoulder. He jerked it free and surged to his feet. He opened his mouth to yell for help.

I was out of time.

I chucked my last blade, counting on my skill and praying for some divine intervention from any god who would listen.

It thunked straight into his neck. His eyes flared wide as he thudded to his knees.

I watched him fall, grateful for once that my magic was worthless. It would have been useless with my wrists bound in these dampening cuffs, and not having it all these years forced me to be good at fighting. These guards clearly weren't expecting prisoners to fight back with their hands.

"Hurry!" the kid hissed. "I hear someone!"

"Get in here!" I whispered. The buzzer that had woken the sleeping guard had been too quiet to be a building-wide alarm. Just one to wake him in case of visitors.

At least, I hoped.

The kid slipped inside and shut the door. I kept my ears perked as I rolled the demon over. My hand was drawn straight to his belt where he had a keyring attached. I unclipped it, then tugged the daggers out of the demon.

"Here, kid." I handed him the keys. "Find one that'll fit these cuffs."

It took a couple tries, with me sweating all the while as I

listened to guards passing outside the room, but the kid got me unlocked. I slipped the key ring over my wrist for safekeeping.

By the time the cuffs were off, I figured I'd been gone from the cell ward for about six minutes. We were pushing it. Someone would either find the guards' bodies soon or notice that they'd disappeared.

"I think it's clear," the kid said.

"Let's go." I clutched both daggers and listened one more time at the door, then headed out.

We walked quickly down the hall and pushed our way out into the fight room. I didn't breathe again until we were lost in the crowd, headed back toward the cells.

The guard's body had disappeared by the time we reached the door. We pushed through. The small antechamber was empty, too. So was the hall of cells. As soon as I entered, the sickly emptiness filled my chest. The whole hall was enchanted to repress magic, not just the cuffs. Probably how they kept all these supernaturals contained.

I went straight to Nix's cell, fumbling with the keys.

"Where's my sister's cell?" the kid asked.

"Conner?" Claire called.

The kid raced to her cell. "I'm here to get you out!"

"Idiot! It's dangerous in here."

"Duh. Hang on."

The key snicked in the lock on Nix's door. I turned it just as the kid appeared at my side.

"Give me that," he said as I pushed the door open.

"Hang on," I said as Nix raced into the hall. "Come on, Nix. You can duplicate the key in the next room. Magic isn't repressed there."

We turned to go to the small room where the first guard had stood. It was only two doors down.

"Where are you going?" the kid asked. "Give me the key."

"She can duplicate the key, and we'll get everyone out," I said. "Give us thirty seconds."

He looked torn, but he nodded. Good, because he was no match for me if I wanted something. And I'd see to it his sister got out.

We hurried to the small room, which was still empty, thank magic. The kid followed us.

"Oh, that feels better," Nix said as we stepped out of the corridor and our magic was no longer repressed.

She grabbed the keyring, hovering her hand over the key for the cells. Blue light glowed around her palm as her magic swelled in the air. Her eyes squeezed tight in concentration.

A new key fell to the ground, then another and another. She was going for quantity, which I applauded. I didn't want to leave anyone in this hellhole, and we needed numbers if we were going to escape.

The kid reached down and grabbed a couple keys, then raced off to his sister's cell. Nix duplicated a dozen cell keys. When she removed her hand, her face was wan.

"You used too much power," I said.

"Nah. Let's get these folks out."

We gathered up the keys and headed back into the cell corridor.

The door to Claire's cell burst open as we ran to the next door. She hugged her brother, then caught my eye. "Thanks!"

"Anytime," I said. "Help us get the rest out."

I didn't know what kinds of supernaturals were locked up in this place, but even if they were dangerous, they weren't worse than the guards. And odds were, they'd be on our side.

I shoved a key into a lock and yanked open the door. A middle-aged man rushed out, and I shoved a spare key into his hand.

"Help us get the others out."

He nodded, his eyes wide. "Anything. Thank you."

We raced through the hall, unlocking doors and handing off keys. Some ran for it immediately; others stayed to help. All looked like hell. I revised my opinion about Claire having been here a long time. The ones who'd been here a long time *really* looked like it. Skinny and beat up.

Hot rage welled in my chest, making my heart thud loud in my ears. I'd kill that bastard Arturo. And I wanted to kill every asshole out in the stadium, jeering at the fight ring.

Nix ran up to me. "That's everyone in this hall. All the doors are open."

"Good, let's get out of here." We ran for the main door, flowing out on a tide of freed prisoners. The kid and his sister ran at my side.

"Any other cells?" I asked Claire.

"Don't think so. Just this hall."

"Good." We burst through the doors into the main fight room. My magic was released from the binding spell that had cloaked the cell ward, filling my chest with warmth. I might not be able to use my magic, but that didn't mean I liked when it was suppressed.

Two of the prisoners pushed away from our group, headed straight for the fight ring. They threw out their hands, and their magic surged. Heat singed my skin.

The metal cage around the fight ring melted, molten metal pouring to the ground.

Whoa. I'd bet these guys hadn't been allowed to use that talent during their stint in the fights. Metal burned through the wooden supports holding up the fight ring. The crowd shrieked and stumbled over itself to get away. The wolf and bear who'd been in the cage leapt over the melted metal and raced to join the mages who'd freed them.

Guards charged us, but it didn't really matter now that all the prisoners were free to use their magic. They were more than a match for the guards, as long as we stuck together. Magic surged on the air, a hundred different signatures.

I focused on my dragon sense, calling up my desire to find Del.

"This way!" I shouted to Nix.

We parted from the crowd, leaving them to escape on their own. With their powers accessible, they'd be fine. Nix and I pushed our way through the crowd, which was going the other way, toward the exit.

"Where're you going?"

I turned to see the kid running next to me, his sister at his side.

"To save my other sister," I said. "Get out of here. It's not safe."

"We'll help you. I wouldn't have gotten Claire without you."

"All right." I'd take whatever help was offered, if it meant saving Del.

We shoved our way through the crowd to the other side of the huge room. My dragon sense pulled me to a pair of fancy wooden doors, much nicer than the basic metal that demarcated the guards' chambers and the cells.

"She's through here." I shoved the door open and raced down the hall, pulled toward the room at the end.

I drew a dagger from my boot and kicked the door open. A small crowd—three men and two women—sat at a round table in front of a fireplace. Del was bound, sitting on the floor in front of Arturo.

I raised my knife to hurl it at his awful face, but a blast of fire streaked by me from behind, heating the side of my face. The flame engulfed Arturo. He screamed, throwing himself to the rug. Claire lunged in front of me, throwing another blast of flame.

"You bastard!" she shrieked as she lit him up like a bonfire.

The four seated at the table surged to their feet.

I flung my dagger at the man whose magic smelled like rotten apples. It pierced him in the eye. The other three stood, one woman throwing an enormous icicle.

I dodged just in time. It crashed into the wall behind me and shattered, throwing tiny shards of ice at my arms and legs. The kid hurled his acid bomb, hitting icicle girl right in the face. The acid raced over her body, covering her completely. She didn't even have time to scream before she dropped to the floor.

Oookay, the kid was scarier than he looked.

Claire turned her fire on the other two at the table, lighting them up in an inferno. They fell to the ground, blackened as charcoal.

I ran to Del, pulling the key out of my pocket and undoing her shackles.

"Are you okay?" I asked.

"Yeah, yeah. They were just trying to convince me to use teleportation to abduct more fighters."

"Convince?"

"They hadn't gotten to the tough stuff yet. I think they hire that out."

Tough stuff, as in *torture.* I was glad they were dead.

I looked up to see Claire nudging Arturo's body with her boot.

"Thanks for the help," I said.

"Thanks for getting me out of there. And I wanted a piece of this bastard."

"So, did we just bring down his operation, or what?" I didn't like the idea of this place existing.

"Yeah. These were his closest colleagues, from what I saw. At least, they sat with him in the fancy box during the fights." She glanced at Connor, who'd walked up to her and rubbed her shoulder. "And thanks for taking care of my brother."

"Hey, I could handle myself," he said.

I glanced at the acid-covered body of the woman he'd bombed. He might look young, but yeah, he could handle himself.

"With this jerk dead, there's no one to pay the demon guards, right?"

"I figure," Claire said.

"Good. Then let's get out of here. Maybe you can torch it on your way out."

She grinned.

"Where are we, anyway?" Del asked as we walked out of the room.

"Oregon," Conner said. "About a hundred miles outside of Magic's Bend. In the wilderness."

"Magic's Bend? The biggest all-magic city in America?" I asked. They'd transported us a long way.

"Yeah. We moved there about a year ago. Great place. You should come visit."

I glanced at Nix and Del as we walked out into the bright sunlight. It was a beautiful day.

"Why not?" Del said.

"Sounds good to me," Nix said.

We were free, after all. OMB was dead.

"Yeah, we will," I said. Might as well get started on having a real life, now that we were free.

Then I thought of OMB and his rooms full of treasure. And the fact that we still needed to buy concealment charms to hide from the unnamed monster who hunted us. "We've got something we need to do, but maybe we'll swing by some day."

EPILOGUE

Two months later

"I already like it here." I stepped out of the car.

The massive, refurbished factory building rose four stories tall in front of us. It was made of a warm red brick and dotted with dozens of glittering windows.

Cute shops were on the bottom level, including our new friends Conner and Claire's coffee shop, Potions & Pastilles. There was a park on the other side of the street, and the Oregon summer morning was bright and cool. Birds chirped, welcoming us to the neighborhood.

"And we have OMB to thank for it," Del said.

Nix laughed. "Yeah. In a roundabout way."

After leaving the fight ring two months ago, we'd gone straight to OMB's home and base of operations. Word had just gotten out amongst his minions that he was dead, so the place had been in chaos. We'd used the opportunity to steal most of his treasures—the greedy bastard had kept a lot of it instead of selling—and we'd fenced some of it to get the cash to rent this place on Factory Row, in Magic's Bend, Oregon.

We were starting over. OMB hadn't had any family and no loyal workers—the downside of blackmailing your staff into working for you—so it was unlikely anyone was coming for us.

And if they were, they couldn't find us even if they wanted to. The first thing we'd bought with our stolen loot was concealment charms. Anyone who sought us with the intent to do us harm would come up blank.

I grabbed my duffel bag out of the trunk of the old car I'd bought with our leftover funds and tossed Del and Nix's bags to them. They snagged them, and we set off across the street toward our new home.

"The sign guy should be here in a couple hours," I said.

The bottom row of all the buildings on Factory Row were glass-fronted shops. Ours was one of them.

"Ancient Magic." Del waved her hands toward the area over the glass door that led into the empty retail space that would become our shop. "I like it."

"Me too. I never liked that OMB sold the artifacts we found." It just felt wrong. Like stealing history. Of the treasures we'd stolen from him, we'd sold the modern jewelry to buy this place, so I didn't feel too guilty about that.

"I think we've got a good business model," Nix said. She'd been reading up these last couple months on how to run a small business. "We provide something unique and valuable, but legal."

"Barely," I said.

But Del, who'd always been good with books, had done all our research and determined that our plan was on the right side of the law. Which was good, because we didn't want to end up on the wrong side of the Order of the Magica.

It'd taken us a month to sort it out and figure out exactly how we'd make a living now that we weren't controlled by OMB. But we'd come up with something great At least, as far as I was concerned.

Ancient Magic would sell the charms and spells that were trapped in enchanted artifacts. We each had a role to play, and had come up with cool nicknames because we're giant nerds. Del was the Seeker. Using old texts, she would identify the artifacts and the magic that we would sell. I was the Huntress—the best name out of the bunch, if you asked me. I'd use my dragon sense to find the artifacts in the tombs and temples, and I'd retrieve them. Nix was the Protector. She'd work in the shop and protect our wares. But more importantly, she'd conjure replicas of the artifacts and transfer the magic to them. That's what we would sell—the replicas and the magic, not the artifact. I would then return the artifact to its original resting place.

The part that kept us on the right side of the law was that we would only choose artifacts that held enchantments that were nearly expired. All magic decays with time. If it's trapped in an object, it can become volatile. Explosions, spells gone awry, and other problems can occur. We were like a cleanup crew, but we took care of the problems before they started. And sold them.

At least, that was the plan. I had high hopes it would work out.

I pressed my face against glass door and peered inside.

"Empty and boring," I said. "But that'll change."

"Good thinking to jumpstart our stock with OMB's collection," Del said.

"Thanks." I grinned.

In addition to the jewelry, we'd stolen OMB's archaeological treasures, but I'd hesitated to sell them for cash. It was that dilemma which had sparked this idea. While we'd been waiting for the paperwork to close on our new shop and apartments, Nix had practiced her conjuring and magic transfer, creating the bulk of our stock. I'd returned the artifacts to their original resting places, most of which I had known because I'd been the one to steal them in the first place. The car was packed full of the stuff, ready to go on the shelves.

"What do you say we check out our apartments?" I said. We'd bought the whole top three floors of the building over the shop—one for each of us.

"Sure," Del said.

"Hey, guys!" Conner's voice echoed down the street.

I turned to see him and Claire headed our way. We'd moved to Magic's Bend because of them. After escaping the fight ring, we'd kept in touch. They'd painted a nice picture of the place. And it'd been a good choice, anyway. It was the biggest all-magic city in America—the perfect place to set up our shop.

"Hey!" Nix said.

Conner and Claire stopped in front of us. Conner carried a little paper tray of coffees, and Claire had a brown paper bag in her hand. They thrust them out.

"Welcome gift," Claire said. "My brother's excellent scones and coffee."

I grinned and took the coffees. "Thanks."

Del dug into the bag and shoved most of a scone into her mouth. I laughed, but Conner's baked goods *were* amazing. One of the major perks of living on Factory Row was our proximity to Potions & Pastilles and their awesome assortment of goodies.

Another perk was our proximity to friends. We'd never had friends before. Or a place of our own. Or freedom.

Now, we had all three. And I couldn't wait to see what we'd do with it.

~~~

Thanks for reading! Turn the page for an excerpt of *Ancient Magic*, the next book in the series.

THANK YOU FOR READING!

I hope you enjoyed reading this book as much as I enjoyed writing it. Reviews are *so* helpful to authors. I really appreciate all reviews, both positive and negative. If you want to leave one, you can do so on Amazon or Goodreads.

Turn the page for an excerpt of *Ancient Magic*, Cass's next book.

EXCERPT OF ANCIENT MAGIC

PROLOGUE

Five Years Before The Events in Southeast Asia & The Fight Ring

Blood. I rubbed my tongue against the top of my mouth. Definitely blood. Fear shivered through me. The ground scratched my bare arms and the back of my neck. Prickly grass? My eyelids were gritty as I lifted them and blinked into the darkness. Stars twinkled down.

Night? Where was I?

Panic closed my throat. I gasped for air.

I pushed myself up and looked down. A ragged dress covered my skinny form, but didn't protect me from the chill night. I shivered as cold embraced me. A battered golden locket lay on my chest. It looked old, but I didn't recognize it.

A field stretched out around me, illuminated by starlight and a moon that hung low over the earth. The hair on my arms stood up at the sound of night creatures in the distance. A cold breeze rustled the grass, but fear chilled me more than the wind. Why was I out here?

Please don't let me be alone.

LINSEY HALL

My heart thundered in my ears as I glanced around.

Two girls who looked to be about fourteen or fifteen lay sprawled on the ground beside me. They wore ragged dresses like mine.

Why was I here with two other girls my age?

Wait—were they my age? When I thought about it, I couldn't remember how old I was exactly. Just trying to think of it sent an icepick of pain through my skull.

With a trembling hand, I reached out and shook the girl closest to me.

"Wake up," I said. Panic sunk its claws into my chest. Why were we here?

When she didn't wake, I shouted, "Wake up!"

The girl gasped and shot upright, her black hair stuck with grass. Her terrified blue eyes met mine.

"Run," she gasped.

She spoke Irish, like I did, and the word shot straight through me.

"Hide," I said. "We have to hide."

I wasn't sure why, but I knew it more strongly than I knew anything else in the world. Her word—*run*—had triggered my own. *Hide.*

"Get up!" I scrambled to my feet. "We have to hide. Now. Now, now, now."

She clambered up, and we frantically tugged at the arms of the girl who still lay on her back. She was so pale she looked dead.

But I couldn't leave her. "Get up!"

She shrieked and jerked out of our hold, then crouched like a terrified animal. Her dark hair hung in her face.

What had happened to her, to us, that we were like this?

"FireSoul," she whispered, also in Irish. Her wide green gaze met mine through the curtain of hair.

The fear in her eyes must have mirrored my own. Her word pricked at my consciousness, but fear overrode it.

My heart pounded in my chest, trying to break my ribs. "Come on. We have to hide!"

She nodded and her head whipped around, searching for shelter like a cornered animal. I looked too. A small patch of woods about a hundred yards behind me caught my eye.

"This way." I spun and set off running across the field. They followed.

My lungs burned and my legs ached as we raced. I clearly wasn't used to being outside, nor to exercise.

But why? When I tried to think of the reason, nothing came but pain. My head ached when I tried to remember myself or my past. A sob burst from my chest. I couldn't remember anything.

Fear and the desperate need to hide drove me on when I wanted to stop and collapse to the ground, weeping. The trees loomed ahead—leafless, claw-like branches reaching for the sky. They were terrifying, but far better than the open field.

There was nowhere to hide in an open field.

Hide.

We dove into the woods, plowing through the underbrush until we were deep in the forest. Night creatures continued to rustle around us.

When we came to a large pile of collapsed trees, I plunged into them. Bark and branches scratched my arms as I found a nook created by the collapsed wood. The other girls crowded in behind me.

They were warm. Familiar, though I didn't recognize them. Safe.

We huddled together, panting. It wasn't quite as dark when they were near me, though it was more a feeling than reality.

Cold pinched my cheeks. I reached up and touched wetness.

Tears.

One of the other girls sniffled.

"What's your name?" I asked.

"It's—" The green-eyed girl started panting. Moonlight illuminated her panic-filled eyes. "I don't know!"

"I don't either!" the other girl cried. "I don't know my name!"

I tried to think of my own, poking for memories.

Pain.

I didn't know how old I was. Or where I was from. It hadn't been a fluke before. I really couldn't remember. "I don't know anything either!"

We gasped and cried, huddling closer. Their warmth felt familiar, like we'd done this a hundred times before. Slowly, it soothed me. I tried reaching into my mind to draw out some memories.

"Ouch." I cringed.

"What's wrong?" asked the dark-haired girl.

"Every time I try to remember something, my head hurts."

"Me too," said the green-eyed girl.

"And me," sniffled the other.

"Then what do we remember?"

"Run," said the dark-haired girl. "We're running, but I don't know from what."

"Is that how we got into the field?" I asked.

"Maybe." Her voice shook. "*Run* was all I remembered. When I woke, it was the only thing in my mind."

"*Hide*," I said, thinking back. "That's what I remembered. We must hide. From a bad man." I rubbed my temple. "Or woman? From someone very bad."

Just the shadowy memory made tears pour down my face. My shoulders shook. The trembling traveled down my arms and legs until my entire body quaked.

I couldn't remember who we were hiding from, but my body remembered. Hiding from evil. Bad. *Bad, bad, bad.*

The green-eyed girl threw her arms around me. "Hey, hey, calm down. It'll be okay."

I gasped through my sobs and realized I'd been saying *bad* out loud. I didn't believe that it'd be okay—not really—but her words made me feel a little better.

"What do you remember?" I asked.

"FireSoul," she whispered. "We are FireSouls."

I gasped and jerked out of her arms. "No, we're not. We can't be."

I might not have remembered my own past, but some knowledge of the world still seemed to be intact. FireSouls were bad. Even the word sent a shiver of panic through me.

Run, hide, and *FireSoul* were my only memories? That couldn't be. In my mind, I poked for the biggest, most important pieces of information. I wanted to know something.

What came was that I lived in a world full of magic. Thoughts burst in my mind. "I'm one of the Magica—you two feel like Magica as well."

I could feel their power now that I tried. Could smell it and taste it. The green-eyed girl's power felt like water on my skin and smelled like flowers. Tasted like vanilla. The dark-haired girl was just as powerful. Her magic felt like soft grass beneath my feet and smelled like fresh laundry. It tasted sweet, but I couldn't place it.

"Magica?" the dark-haired girl asked.

"Magica can create magic!" the green-eyed girl said, excitement in her voice. "I remember now. But I don't remember what kind I am. Witch, or sorcerer, or… mage."

"Or shifter, demon, or fairy," I added as the memories flowed back. "But they aren't Magica. They are supernaturals like us, but they don't use magic the same way we do. But they know about us. Unlike humans. The Great Peace keeps us hidden." It came back to me in pieces. Though we lived alongside humans, the Great Peace—the most powerful bit of magic ever created—hid us from human eyes. It took the powerful spells of hundreds of Magica and shifters to create the Great Peace. "Humans can see us but not our magic, which we shouldn't use around them anyway."

"Right, I remember now," the dark-haired girl said.

"I feel your power too. But you don't feel evil," I said. "Not like a FireSoul would feel."

"We're not evil," the green-eyed girl said. "We haven't killed...I don't think. But I do remember that we're FireSouls. I know it."

"Everyone hates FireSouls," I whispered. They were the bogeyman because they stole the magical gifts of others by killing the original owner. Was *I* the bogeyman? Me and these two girls? Had I killed another Magica to steal his gift? Wouldn't I remember something as terrible as that?

"Is that why we're hiding?" the dark-haired girl asked. "Are we hiding from the Order of the Magica and the Alpha Council?"

"No," I said, though the two supernatural governing organizations would be after us if they knew we were FireSouls. "We're hiding from someone worse. But if we really are FireSouls, we can't tell anyone. They'll throw us in prison."

"We are FireSouls," she said. "When I woke, I knew it. It was my memory. As strong as yours."

I swallowed hard, remembering how strong that urge to hide had been. I'd woken confused, but when the dark-haired girl had said *run*, it had burst back into my consciousness.

"Are we really FireSouls?" the dark-haired girl asked. "I don't feel like a FireSoul. I don't feel evil."

I didn't either. I felt hungry and cold. My stomach growled and I shivered. If only I had something to eat. If only I was warm. I wanted it so badly.

A strange feeling tugged at my middle. As if there were a string tied around my waist that pulled me to the left. A sense of food and warmth flowed from the invisible string.

"There's food and shelter nearby," I said. "I feel it."

"Treasure," whispered the green-eyed girl. "You can sense treasure."

Treasure. Of course I could sense food and shelter. I coveted them. They were treasure to me right now.

I was a FireSoul. That was proof.

FireSouls were given that name because they shared a piece of a dragon's soul, though no one knew how it had happened. If dragons still existed, they were hiding. But legend said that all magic descended from dragons. FireSouls somehow shared a part of their soul.

That's why we could steal powers and find treasure. Dragons were covetous. They coveted treasure of all varieties—including the powers of others. The greatest treasure of all could only be obtained through death.

"We can find what we need with our dragon-sense," said the green-eyed girl. "If we want it badly enough, it becomes treasure. Then we follow our sense to it."

Was that how we were supposed to survive? Become hungry enough to find food and then steal it?

I looked down at my ragged dress and skinny body. The only thing I had of value was the necklace, and even that was probably almost worthless. It didn't look like I had a lot of choice right now. If I had parents, I had no idea who they were or how to find them.

My throat tightened. Did I have a mom and dad? Where were they? I pushed through the pain in my mind, trying to remember. But nothing came. Just blinding agony. I slumped against the other girls.

"Are you okay?" one asked.

"Yes." I pushed thoughts of parents away and focused on surviving. "If we use our dragon sense, we have to be careful."

If we were caught, we would be thrown in the Prison for Magical Miscreants. It was a cold, dark, terrible place, I remembered that. A shiver ran over me. My own personal bogeyman. In the corner of my mind, it felt like someone had once threatened me with that prison, but when I poked at the memory, the blinding pain came again. Why didn't I learn? I needed to quit poking at my personal past.

"We need names," I said.

"Yes. I hate not having one," said the dark-haired girl.

The green-eyed girl looked up at the sky. "I will be Phoenix. After the constellation. Call me Nix."

I liked that. Naming ourselves for something bigger gave me hope. I looked up too. A cluster of bright stars caught my eye. I didn't know what in my past had taught me the constellations, but I was grateful for it. "I'll be Cassiopeia. Call me Cass."

The green-eyed girl looked up and sighed. "You took the best ones."

I giggled, the sound surprising me.

"I'll take Delphinus," she said finally. "But it'll be Delphine. And you can call me Del."

"Okay. Del and Nix." They both looked so different. Panic gripped my throat as I realized that I didn't know what I looked like. I pulled my hair around. Red. "We look nothing alike. I don't think we're related by blood, even though we're all FireSouls."

They were rare from what I remembered, but I didn't recall the gift being genetic.

"We're sisters now," Nix said. "Because we're all we've got. I don't remember my parents."

"Me neither." Del sniffed back tears.

"We'll find them." I closed my eyes and focused on the idea of parents. I wanted them more than anything, so I should be able to find them.

But the magical string didn't tie itself around my middle. I thought harder, reaching into my mind, pretending it was a book I could flip through.

Agony pierced my skull.

I retreated, gasping.

"I tried to find them," I said. My parents were lost to me. My throat tightened and tears burned. "I don't think I know enough about them. I could imagine food and find that. But people are harder, I think."

"We'll find them somehow," Del said.

I nodded, trying to hope but finding it hard.

"We can only use our dragon sense to find food and other things we need," I said. "No killing for other powers." I didn't want to be a murderer, no matter how much power it got me.

Nix nodded. "I don't want to be a monster."

"Me neither," said Del.

"If another supernatural asks how we can find things, we say we are Seekers," I said.

The green-eyed girl smiled. "That's a good idea. Camouflage ourselves."

"Exactly." Seekers were a type of supernatural who could find things. As long as we didn't kill and steal powers, we could use our ability to find treasure and just say that we were Seekers.

"Do we have other powers we can use?" Del asked.

"I don't know," I said. If it was about me directly, I couldn't seem to remember. "FireSouls can be other types of supernaturals as well. You both feel magical to me."

Nix closed her eyes. I felt her power surge against me like water lapping at my skin. The taste of vanilla burst on my tongue, and her flower scent filled my nose. Her hands began to glow. She cupped them in front of her.

Eventually, a small match appeared in her palms.

"You're a conjurer," I said as my power swelled within me.

"Not a very good one," Nix said. "I wanted to conjure a fire for warmth."

I listened with half an ear as the power in my chest grew. It felt like it was in response to hers, spurred on by what she had. I embraced it, though I didn't understand it, and held my arms out. The magic pulsed within me, roaring to be released. I raised my palms to the sky and let it go.

An enormous fireball shot from my palms, throwing me back

onto the ground as it roared into the sky. It burned away the tops of the trees and exploded into the night. Orange flames surged through the air, burning my skin.

Panic rose in my chest as I scrambled to my feet. We were trapped. Del and Nix looked at me with horrified eyes.

"I don't know what happened!" I said. The sky above me continued to burn, though the forest around us was untouched. "People will see the flame! We have to hide!"

Del lunged for me. She enveloped me in her arms and grabbed Nix, pulling her into the hug. A second later, the ground fell out from under me.

We collapsed to the ground a moment later. It was colder here, the wind stronger. I climbed to my feet. We were on a mountain looking down on the field below. Fire roiled in the air above it, a beacon of magic. But at least it wasn't lower. The animals and the people would be safe.

"We were in a valley," I said as I turned to Del. "And you can transport."

Del's wide eyes met mine. "Apparently. It was instinct. I followed it. And thank magic for it. What did you do down there?"

I looked down at the field that was lighting up the night. It would draw people. We were fine on the mountain for a little while because we were so far away, but we needed to get out of here soon.

"I didn't mean to light it all on fire," I said. "When Nix conjured the match, I felt like I could create a match too. So I let my power out."

"You're a Mirror Mage," Nix said. "You borrowed my conjuring power."

"A strong one," Del said.

"Too strong. I couldn't control it."

Mirror Mages weren't rare or very dangerous, from what I recalled. They could reflect back the magic of any supernatural that they were with. But it was just temporary, and the other supernatural got to keep their powers the whole time. From what I remembered, if Mirror Mages didn't use the borrowed gift right away, they could use it later. But it was a one shot deal. I could have held on to the conjuring gift I'd borrowed from Nix, but I'd only have been able to use it once.

In a way, Mirror Mages were a tiny bit like FireSouls because they used the powers of others. But they weren't very dangerous because they couldn't keep the magic or replicate it more than once.

I turned toward the valley. The fire was starting to dissipate, but it was still an unnatural spectacle, the sky alight with flame.

"I could have killed us if I hadn't pointed my hands to the sky," I whispered. "I'm dangerous."

"I think you need to practice," Del said.

"Or not use my power at all." Tears pricked at my eyes. Why was I like this?

"Let's not worry about that now," Nix said. "We should get out of here. Let's find food and shelter."

I nodded and blinked the tears away. "Okay. Let's go."

We set off along the mountain ridge, following the magical string tied around our waists. I was tired and scared, but at least I had my *deirfiúr*. My sisters.

But as I walked, the most horrible thought occurred to me. Had I been born a Mirror Mage, or had I killed someone for this gift?

CHAPTER ONE

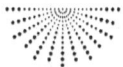

Ten Years Later
Temple of Murreagh
Deep Beneath Western Ireland

"Cass! Answer me, damn it. Are you hurt?" Nix's voice echoed quietly from the pendant around my neck.

"Gimme a sec," I wheezed as I shoved the huge rock off my leg and scrambled behind a big boulder. Pain radiated from my shin, but nothing felt broken, thank magic. I didn't have time to deal with it anyway. A nasty looking shadow demon was currently trying to blow my head off. As long as my limbs were mostly functional, I was good to go.

A blast of magic blew apart the stone over my head.

I ducked and rubble bounced off my shoulders.

Damn demon!

When it stopped, I peered over the boulder at the demon who guarded the altar in the middle of the underground temple. It'd taken me nearly six hours to get through the enchantments that led to the temple. Fire charms, moving rocks, an awful riddle—

the whole lot. Real Indiana Jones stuff, but I didn't have the cool hat.

After all that, it seemed like it should be smooth sailing. But no, this treasure was protected by a shadow demon. Who was apparently very displeased with my presence.

His skin was dark gray, his powerful body clad in simple pants and a shirt. He was basically human-shaped, except for the exceptionally bulky arms and the narrow black horns that came out near his temples and ran back along his skull. Dark eyes glinted maniacally through the dust in the air.

Though big, he was dwarfed by the subterranean temple that housed the Chalice of Youth, my current assignment. The chalice sat on an altar behind the demon, gleaming gold. Graceful columns supported the soaring stone ceiling, each carved in the shape of a different long-forgotten goddess. The only light came from eerie torches that lined the walls. The air was stagnant, permeated by the scent of smoke that wafted from the shadow demon.

"Do I send backup?" Nix asked through static.

"No. I've got this." I didn't usually need my friends to step in and save my butt on a job, but it gave me the warm fuzzies to know they were willing. "You're breaking up, Nix. Too much magic from the demon. I'm turning you off now."

Strong magic, like the kind the demon was throwing, usually interfered with the comms charm that hung around my neck. Something about the magical signature overpowering the puny charm that fueled my necklace.

I usually worked alone, but sometimes—okay, always—a riddle enchantment stumped me. At that point, Nix was there to back me up via a quick call through my comms charm. But now that she'd gotten me through the riddle that had opened the main door to this temple—Why does a dragon cross the road?—I no longer needed her help.

"Fine, don't—" More static broke up Nix's voice.

"If I'm not out in an hour, remember that I hate lilies," I said. "Worst funeral flower."

"But—"

I touched the silver charm around my throat, and its magic went dormant. Only the sound of the shadow demon's breathing echoed in the chamber.

It was time to get this over with. I was starving, and this was my last gig before the long weekend. My leg screamed as I pushed myself to my feet. *Breathe through the pain. It's just bruising.*

I drew my obsidian blades from the sheaths strapped to my thighs and stepped out from behind the boulder. Torchlight reflected wickedly off the black volcanic glass. Lefty and Righty, I called them—not nearly regal enough names for their power— but I'd never been good at clever names.

"Time to go back to hell, fella," my voice echoed in the stone chamber. "The devil says he's missin' ya."

The shadow demon laughed, his dark gray skin absorbing the light. Fine, it was a little corny, but I was tired.

The demon raised his hand to throw another blast of magic at me. I flung Righty at him, dodging the whoosh of magic that he managed to get off before my blade sunk into his arm.

Perfect hit. Ten points.

He roared in pain as heat seared my shoulder through my leather jacket.

Oh, so he wanted to play that way? With heat as well as wind? I thought wistfully of blasting him back with a reflection of his own power. His magic manifested as burning smoke. I'd give him a flaming tornado.

Except that was the problem. My magic was too powerful for me to control. I just blew shit up if I tried. I didn't want to draw attention to myself, so I didn't use my power. But I didn't hide that I was a Mirror Mage—strong supernaturals could tell I had magic. If I didn't use it often, my magical signature appeared weak to those strong enough to sense others' powers.

So I'd gotten really good with weapons.

I pricked the back of my hand with Lefty before immediately throwing the blade at the demon's heart. My blood ignited a spell that would call its twin back to me.

As Lefty hurtled toward the demon, Righty pulled itself out of the demon's arm and flew through the air toward me. As long as I was quick—which I usually was—I always had a dagger at hand.

I reached up and snagged Righty as I kept an eye on the dagger that zoomed toward the demon. He used magic to blast it away.

"That's all you've got?" he roared.

I dove behind the nearest column, a stone warrior woman in a flowing cloak, both of her hands gripping swords.

A guardian. Of me, I decided.

I swiped my dagger over the small amount of blood welling on the back of my hand so that my other blade returned to me.

The demon roared again, his muscles bulging beneath his thin shirt as he drew his arms back to throw twin blasts of magic at me. All supernaturals had different gifts and his seemed to be throwing blazing blasts of smoke that blew things apart like a grenade.

The smoke blast hit my guardian column. Her bottom half blew apart, rock and debris flying across the temple. With an enormous cracking sound, the guardian crashed to the ground. The stone floor vibrated beneath my feet. Dust filled the air until I could hardly see.

Guilt ate at me over the damage done to such an ancient place. Don't worry about that now. Fix it later. I jumped onto the guardian, who was now lying on the ground in several large pieces, all lined up in a row. I raced across her skirt, jumping from piece to piece until I was right above the shadow demon.

I leapt for him.

He looked up at the last moment, his eyes widening. He twisted and Lefty sank into his meaty shoulder. With a roar, he threw me off him. I skidded across the floor, then groped my way behind the top of the fallen column. He was strong, both in magic and form, and his magic smelled ancient. Like dust. I'd bet he was an old demon.

"Blades?" he yelled. "You come at me with blades? Use your magic and give me a real fight!"

"What? You bored? Been guarding this tomb a long time, eh?" I said as I flung Righty at him.

It sank into his chest, nearly a perfect shot at his heart. Or at least, where I figured a shadow demon's heart might be.

He yanked it out and said, "You have no idea."

I swallowed hard.

Missed his heart, I guess.

Quickly, before he could fling the dagger, I called it back to me. Righty pulled itself out of the demon's hand and flew home.

The demon didn't startle, nor did he look weakened by the dark blood leaking from the wound in his chest. Old and strong, like I'd thought. Even if I hadn't hit his heart, he should at least be incapacitated. But this one was different. He wasn't even winded from the blade that had sunk six inches into his chest.

"Well? Won't you give me a real fight? You are one of the three. Strong enough to fight, but you don't."

My heart tried to climb into my throat. "What does that mean?"

The three? Did he mean me and my *deirfiúr*? How could he know about Del and Nix?

"What do you mean?" I screamed when he didn't answer quickly enough.

"You don't use your powers." He threw another blast of magic at me. Blazing smoke blasted away my column barricade, and I scrambled back.

He wouldn't use his powers either if it meant getting locked up in the Prison for Magical Miscreants. As long as I didn't use them, I could pretend that I was nothing but a low-strength

Mirror Mage and have a lovely life where no one tossed me in prison.

The shadow demon threw another blast of fiery smoke. It plowed into the ground in front of me. The stone floor exploded. The blast threw me backwards. Pain streaked through me. My entire front felt singed, pierced by small pieces of shattered stone. A cough tore through my lungs and I blinked blindly, my throat and eyes burning.

I could barely see, and he kept throwing those damned blasts of smoke at me, driving me ever backward. I just had to get him to lay off for a sec. Then I could question him.

Through the dust, I could make out his hulking form approaching. It was risky, but I threw each of my blades in quick succession, hoping to incapacitate but not kill.

The thud of a body collapsing sounded. The blasts of power stopped coming.

I climbed to my feet and limped toward the form sprawled on the ground. The stone bit into my knees when I dropped beside him. My blades protruded from his chest, one embedded in each pectoral. His breath strangled in and out of his lungs, but he wasn't dead. I grasped his rough shirt and shook him.

"What do you know about me?" I said.

"What"—he coughed—"you are."

"But—"

His lips parted, and I snapped my mouth shut, frantic to hear what he had to say.

"FireSoul."

I stumbled back, my stomach twisting. Chills raced over me. How could he know that? No one knew that but my *deirfiúr*.

"I'm a Mirror Mage." My voice came out hardly louder than a whisper. I tried again, louder, fear choking my throat. "I'm a Mirror Mage!"

Panic welled in me, and I crawled back to him, reaching for his shirt again, desperate to shake answers from him.

His eyes were dimming, their gleaming black light turning a dark gray. A great breath shuddered out of his lungs, followed by stillness.

The light faded from his eyes, and his body disappeared. My blades, no longer embedded in a chest, clattered to the floor.

"No!"

My heart threatened to break my ribs. I hit the ground, frustration and fear beating in my chest.

The demon was gone. Not dead—you couldn't really kill a demon—just send them back to whatever hell they'd originally come from. Normally very neat and tidy. Except this one had information about me, and my blades had been too accurate. The demon had seemed so strong when my first blade had found its mark. I'd wanted to question him more. This was what happened when I freaked out. Like a bull in a china shop. And it was the main reason I could never use my magic.

My breath echoed too loudly in my ears. Think, think. How could the demon have known that I was a FireSoul? Was it because this job was in Ireland, my homeland? At least, what I assumed was my homeland, given that I could speak Irish and had red hair.

One option was so terrifying I couldn't even poke it with my mind. It was the bogeyman that lurked at the corner of my memories. Whenever I pressed too hard, it leapt up, bringing with it a splitting headache and adrenaline like nobody would believe.

I had to get out of there. Talk to Nix.

Quickly, I grabbed my blades, shoved them into their sheaths, then climbed to my feet. I limped to the altar, pain singing up my leg, and grabbed the golden chalice. It's magic sang beneath my palm, an unsteady beat that indicated this was old magic. The perfect age for selling. There were other priceless objects too, no doubt tributes to the gods carved onto the columns.

My fingers itched to pocket a couple, namely a golden dagger encrusted with rubies and a strange hexagonal blade that looked wickedly sharp on all sides. Despite my terror, covetousness surged within me. My hand trembled as I reached toward the golden dagger. Just one touch. I wouldn't take it.

No.

I sucked in a deep breath and clenched my fist. Not mine. Not mine. Like an addict resisting a fix, I dragged my gaze away from the glitter.

With a shaking hand, I pulled a small black rock out of an inner jacket pocket. My last transport charm. Like all magic that wasn't my own, they were expensive and hard to come by. Del could make them because she could transport, but her power was limited and they commanded a lot of it, so she couldn't make them often.

I should use the charm only in emergencies.

But this sure felt like a heck of an emergency.

I threw the stone to the ground. It shattered and a glittering silver cloud rose in front of me. I stepped into the sparkling stuff and envisioned my home. Magic grabbed me around the waist and threw me through the ether.

~~~

Ancient Magic is now available on Amazon.

AUTHOR'S NOTE

Hey, there! I hope you enjoyed reading *Hidden Magic*. I've been wanting to write a story about Cass, Nix, and Dell before they started their shop, Ancient Magic, and this seemed like the perfect story to tell. If you've read any of my other books, you might know that I'm also an archaeologist. If you're familiar with archaeology, you might have noticed that Cass does some things that archaeologists would disapprove of: namely, breaking into temples and stealing things. That is fairly high on an archaeologist's list of *Bad Things To Do At An Archaeological Site*. Top of the list, really.

In this Author's Note, I talk a bit about the archaeology/treasure hunting aspect of *Hidden Magic* and about the specific archaeological sites in featured in this book. Skip to the end if you just want to read a few details about the sites and archaeology in *Hidden Magic*. I wrote about the archaeology and treasure hunting in the Author's Note for the other Dragon's Gift books, so this might be repetitive if you've read those (feel free to quit now if so), but I want to include it in each of my Author's Notes because it's so important to me.

So—let's talk about the archaeology and treasure hunting

conundrum. As a kid, I loved history, Indiana Jones, and Laura Croft. When I started writing novels, it was only a matter of time before I applied my love of archaeology and history to my stories.

Hence, Dragon's Gift was born. However, I knew I had a careful line to tread when writing these books. As I'm sure you know, archaeology isn't quite like Indiana Jones (for which I'm both grateful and bitterly disappointed). Sure, it's exciting and full of travel. However, booby-traps are not as common as I expected. Total number of booby-traps I have encountered in my career: zero. Still hoping, though.

When I talk about treading a line with these books, I mean the line between archaeology and treasure hunting. There is a big difference between these two activities. As much as I value arti-facts, they are not treasure. Not even the gold artifacts. They are pieces of our history that contain valuable information, and as such, they belong to all of us. Every artifact that is excavated should be properly conserved and stored in a museum so that everyone can have access to our history (this is an ideal scenario, but why not hope for the ideal?). No one single person can own history, and I believe very strongly that individuals should not own artifacts. Treasure hunting is the pursuit of artifacts for personal gain.

So why did I make Cass Cleraux a treasure hunter? I'd have loved to call her an archaeologist, but nothing about Cass's work is like archaeology. Archaeology is a very laborious, painstaking process—and it certainly doesn't involve selling artifacts. That wouldn't work for the fast paced, adventurous series that I had planned for Dragon's Gift. Not to mention the fact that dragons are famous for coveting treasure. Considering where Cass got her skills from, it just made sense to call her a treasure hunter (though I really like to think of her as a magic hunter).

Even though I write urban fantasy, I strive for accuracy. Cass doesn't engage in archaeological practices—therefore, I cannot call her an archaeologist. I also have a duty as an archaeologist to properly represent my field and our goals—namely, to protect and share history. Treasure hunting doesn't do this. One of the biggest battles that archaeology faces today is protecting cultural heritage from thieves.

During the events in *Hidden Magic*, Cass is literally just a thief. She steals because she is being blackmailed into doing so. Her life is literally on the line. She doesn't like causing damage to the temples, but she does it because otherwise, she and the two people she loves most will end up dead or in prison.

However, once Cass, Del, and Nix open their shop Ancient Magic, they become the masters of their own fates. They make the decisions, right or wrong, and are responsible for their actions. Since this is where the majority of the series takes place, I had to debate long and hard about what Cass would do.

I wanted it to involve all the cool things we think about when we think about archaeology—namely, the Indiana Jones stuff, whether it's real or not. Because that stuff is fun, and my main goal is to write a fun book. But I didn't know quite how to do that while still staying within the bounds of my own ethics. I can cut myself and other writers some slack because this is fiction, but I couldn't go too far into smash and grab treasure hunting.

I consulted some of my archaeology colleagues to get their take, which was immensely helpful. Wayne Lusardi, the State Maritime Archaeologist for Michigan, and Douglas Inglis and Veronica Morris, both archaeologists for Interactive Heritage, were immensely helpful with ideas. My biggest problem was figuring out how to have Cass steal artifacts from tombs and then sell them and still sleep at night. Everything I've just said is pretty counter to this, right?

That's where the magic comes in. Cass isn't after the artifacts themselves (she puts them back where she found them, if you recall)—she's after the magic that the artifacts contain. She's more of a magic hunter than a treasure hunter. That solved a big part of my problem. At least she was putting the artifacts back.

Though that's not proper archaeology (especially the damage she sometimes causes, which she always goes back to fix), I could let it pass. At least it's clear that she believes she shouldn't keep the artifact or harm the site. But the SuperNerd in me said, "Well, that magic is part of the artifact's context. It's important to the artifact and shouldn't be removed and sold."

Now *that* was a problem. I couldn't escape my SuperNerd self, so I was in a real conundrum. Fortunately, that's where the immensely intelligent Wayne Lusardi came in. He suggested that the magic could have an expiration date. If the magic wasn't used before it decayed, it could cause huge problems. Think explosions and tornado spells run amok. It could ruin the entire site, not to mention possibly cause injury and death. That would be very bad.

So now you see why Cass Clereaux and her *deirfiúr* came up with their business model of selling the destructive magic and replacing the artifacts. Not only is selling the magic cooler, it's also better from an ethical standpoint, especially if the magic was going to cause problems in the long run. These aren't perfect solutions—the perfect solution would be sending in a team of archaeologists to carefully record the site and remove the dangerous magic—but that wouldn't be a very fun book. Hopefully this was a good compromise that you enjoyed (and that my old professors don't hang their heads over).

Now, for a bit of the history and archaeology that I use in this book. As with my other books, I included historical sites in *Hidden Magic*. The temple that Cass, Nix, and Del raid is based off the Cambodian temple Angkor Wat. Initially, the Khmer Empire built it as a Hindu temple, but it gradually transformed into a Buddhist temple by the end of the 12th century AD. I briefly mention the Hindu and Buddhist construction elements in the book, but I don't go into them in detail. I don't like the idea of Cass raiding real-life religious monuments, which is why the temples and tombs that I write are always said to be built by supernaturals. The supernaturals who built the temple may have been Hindu or Buddhist—I don't know, it was a long time ago and I like to preserve the mystery for myself, even though I write the books and should know everything:-) But I write from Cass's perspective, and she wouldn't know exactly what the people back then believed, so I don't dwell on it too much myself. Though I can say for sure that they were influenced by the surrounding culture because they built the temple with Hindu and Buddhist influences.

The real-life Angkor Wat is the largest religious monument in the world and is an amazing place. Google it or go to my Pinterest page (click here or search Linsey Hall) to see some pictures. It's riveting.

The Dvarapala is a gate guardian frequently found at Hindu and Buddhist temples across southeast Asia. *Dvala* is from the Sanskrit word *dvāra*, which means gate, and *pala* is from the Sanskrit word *pāla*, which means protector. They are frequently portrayed as a warrior or giant and can have the face of a demon or human. Often, they are armed with the *gadha* mace, though they can carry a sword. They come in many shapes and sizes, from a hulking giant to a more elegant, standing figure. The variety is very impressive and I recommend Googling these as well just to take a peak.

The seven-headed snake that Cass encountered was a variation of the Nāga, the giant serpents or serpent deities found in Buddhist and Hindu mythology. Many southeast Asian countries have a variation of the Nāga in their folklore, though it is different depending upon the country or region. I chose to go with the Cambodian representation because Angkor Wat, the temple I used for inspiration, is based in Cambodia. The Nāga are an important part of Cambodian legend, to the point that their mythology says that they descended from a Nāga princess. In Cambodian iconography, the Nāga often has seven heads. There is a statue of one at the temple of Angkor Wat, which is what I used when creating the giant snake that Cass would face (check out my Pinterest for images).

And finally, the massive trees and roots that are devouring the temple in *Hidden Magic*. They are one of the most distinctive and memorable features at ancient Cambodian temples. The roots have grown up over the buildings and walls, becoming one with the stone (and I don't meant that in an artistic sense). There has been debate over whether or not to remove the trees, but archaeologists determined that it would cause too much damage to the structures. The downside is that the buildings are breaking down faster because of the roots, but it would be too damaging to remove them.

That's pretty much it for the historical and archaeological inspiration for the places in *Hidden Magic*. I hope you enjoyed the book, and thank you for reading!

ACKNOWLEDGMENTS

The Dragon's Gift series is a product of my two lives: one as an archaeologist and one as a novelist. Combining these two took a bit of work. I'd like to thank my friends, Wayne Lusardi, the State Maritime Archaeologist for Michigan, and Douglas Inglis and Veronica Morris, both archaeologists for Interactive Heritage, for their ideas about how to have a treasure hunter heroine that doesn't conflict too much with archaeology's ethics. The Author's Note contains a bit more about this if you are interested

Thank you, Ben, for everything you've done to support me in this career. Thank you to Carol Thomas for sharing your thoughts on the book and being an amazing inspiration.

Thank you to Jena O'Connor and Lindsey Loucks for various forms of editing. The book is immensely better because of you!

GLOSSARY

Conjurer - A Magica who uses magic to create something from nothing. They cannot create magic, but if there is magic around them, they can put that magic into their conjuration.

Dark Magic - The kind that is meant to harm. It's not necessarily bad, but it often is.

Deirfiúr - Sisters in Irish.

Demons - Often employed to do evil. They live in various hells but can be released upon the earth if you know how to get to them and then get them out. If they are killed on earth, they are sent back to their hell.

Dragon Sense - A FireSoul's ability to find treasure. It is an internal sense pulls them toward what they seek. It is easiest to find gold, but they can find anything or anyone that is valued by someone.

Elemental Mage – A rare type of mage who can manipulate all of the elements.

Enchanted Artifacts – Artifacts can be imbued with magic that lasts after the death of the person who put the magic into the artifact (unlike a spell that has not been put into an artifact— these spells disappear after the Magica's death). But magic is not stable. After a period of time—hundreds or thousands of years depending on the circumstance—the magic will degrade. Eventually, it can go bad and cause many problems.

Fire Mage – A mage who can control fire.

FireSoul - A very rare type of Magica who shares a piece of the dragon's soul. They can locate treasure and steal the gifts (powers) of other supernaturals. With practice, they can manipulate the gifts they steal, becoming the strongest of that gift. They are despised and feared. If they are caught, they are thrown in the Prison of Magical Deviants.

Hearth Witch – A Magica who is versed in magic relating to hearth and home. They are often good and potions and protective spells and are also very perceptive when on their own turf.

Magica - Any supernatural who has the power to create magic —witches, sorcerers, mages. All are governed by the Order of the Magica.

Mirror Mage - A Magica who can temporarily borrow the powers of other supernaturals. They can mimick the powers as long as the are near the other supernatural. Or they can hold onto the power, but once they are away from the other supernatural, they can only use it once.

Order of the Magica - There are two governments that enforce law for supernaturals—the Alpha Council and the Order of the Magica. The Order of the Magica govern all Magica. They work cooperatively with Alpha Council when necessary - for example, when capturing FireSouls.

Seeker - A type of supernatural who can find things. FireSouls often pass off their dragon sense as being Seeker power.

Shifter - A supernatural who can turn into an animal. All are governed by the Alpha Council.

Transporter - A type of supernatural who can travel anywhere. Their power is limited and must regenerate after each use.

ABOUT LINSEY

Before becoming a writer, Linsey was an archaeologist who studied shipwrecks in all kinds of water, from the tropics to muddy rivers (and she has a distinct preference for one over the other). After a decade of tromping around in search of old bits of stuff, she settled down to started penning her own adventure novels and is freaking delighted that people seem to like them. Since life is better with a little (or a lot of) magic, she writes urban fantasy and paranormal romance.

This is a work of fiction. All reference to events, persons, and locale are used fictitiously, except where documented in historical record. Names, characters, and places are products of the author's imagination, and any resemblance to actual events, locales, or persons, living or dead, is coincidental.

Linsey@LinseyHall.com
www.LinseyHall.com
https://twitter.com/HiLinseyHall
https://www.facebook.com/LinseyHallAuthor

ISBN 978-1-942085-33-1